BOSE

Also by Larry D. Names:

THE SHAMAN'S SECRET
TWICE DEAD
THE LEGEND OF EAGLE CLAW

BOSE

LARRY D. NAMES

DOUBLEDAY & COMPANY, INC.

GARDEN CITY, NEW YORK

1980

All the characters in this book are fictitious, and any resemblance to actual persons, living or dead, is purely coincidental.

Library of Congress Cataloging in Publication Data

Names, Larry D
  Bose.

  I. Title.
PZ4.N169Bo   [PS3564.A545]   813'.54
ISBN: 0-385-15014-8
Library of Congress Catalog Card Number 79-6283

BOSE

PROLOGUE

It was an old house, constructed during the NRA era of
the '30s. There was a porch on the street side of the struc-
ture and another in the back. The white stucco was chip-
ping away around the foundation, and the steps leading
up to the veranda needed mending. The screens over the
windows and doors were rusted from years of weather.
Pieces of cardboard filled in for the glass that was missing
from some of the windowpanes.

There was more bare earth in the yard than there was
lawn, which suited everyone but the neighbors. What was
left of a picket fence separated the property from the city
sidewalk. The concrete path that led from the street to
the doorstep was cracked, and grass and weeds grew up
through the crevices. In some places, it was plain to see
that the neighborhood dogs favored this piece of real estate.

Two small boys raced into the yard, one wearing an Indian headdress of multicolored feathers and the other
wearing a cowboy hat.

"Bang-bang!" shouted the lad in the brown Stetson. "I
got you, Rafer. You're dead."

Rafer fell to the ground, pretending to be a good Indian, a dead Indian.

An elderly man sat in his rocking chair on the porch,
watching the game of cowboys and Indians being played
by the youngsters. He was more interested in the charade

than most old men might be. He leaned forward in his seat, clucking his tongue at what he was witnessing.

"Rafer!" called the old man. "Bring yo'self up here. I wants to talk to yo'."

Rafer picked himself up from the ground and skipped up the steps, his cowboy friend right behind him.

"Yessuh, Grandpappy," said Rafer. "What yo' wants of me?"

"How comes yo' been playin' cowboys and Injuns and yo' always the Injun?" The old man squinted his eyes at the boy. "Now, yo' answer me that."

"I has to be the Injun, Grandpappy, 'cause I is colored and Tommy is white folks," explained Rafer. "Ev'body knows that cowboys is white folks. They wasn't no black cowboys."

The old man rocked backward, astounded by his grandson's statement. His eyes widened and rolled, and his lips parted in disbelief. Then they closed again, sputtering in their eagerness to say what was on the old man's mind.

"Whatch yo' mean, they wasn't no black cowboys?" spat Grandpappy. "They was plenty of black cowboys. Why, boy, if it wasn't fo' the black cowboys, the Injuns would still be wearin' war paint. Most white folks would still be livin' in the East, too. They was lots of black cowboys in the Old West."

Tommy and Rafer exchanged knowing looks, ones that said that they thought the old gentleman had been too long in the hot sun.

"Now, don't go lookin' like that!" snapped Grandpappy. "I knows what I is sayin'. Now y'all sit yo'selves down, and I'll tell yo' about one black cowboy."

The two boys shrugged their shoulders, but they sat down, just as they had been told.

"I knowed this cowboy when I was a boy," said Grandpappy. "Course, he wasn't a cowboy then, but he was when he was a young man. His name was Bose Ikard. . . ."

ONE

Most folks who talk about the old cattle trails that crossed the plains and mountains, the rivers and deserts, from Texas to the railheads in Kansas, to the mining camps in Colorado, and to the military posts in New Mexico and Arizona never fail to mention the Goodnight-Loving Trail. That hardly seems a proper name for a cattle trail. The designation seems to be more appropriate for a honeymoon road. No matter, though; it was one famous longhorn highway.

When folks talk about it, they sometimes forget one of the men who helped establish this route. His name was Bose Ikard. Most people can't remember him, because he was a Negro, a black man, a black cowboy. Charles Goodnight didn't let Bose slip his mind. The legendary cattle baron always had a fond spot in his heart for him. In fact, when Bose passed away, Goodnight made him immortal by putting up a monument to honor a lifelong friend. Charlie had it inscribed for all to read:

BOSE IKARD

Served with me four years on the Goodnight-Loving Trail, never shirked a duty or disobeyed an order, rode with me in many stampedes, participated in three engagements with Comanches, splendid behavior.

C. Goodnight

Now, that sounds almost as if Charlie were talking more about a faithful horse than a man, but Goodnight had a warmer feeling than that for Bose. After all, Bose had saved his life on more than one occasion.

Bose started out life in typical fashion for Negroes born in the 1840s and '50s. He was a slave, the son of slaves owned by the Ikard family of Mississippi. Although they lived in bondage, Amos and Sheba could still feel the pride and joy of parenthood when they were blessed with their only son, in 1847.

The Ikards, seeing that their future in their native state was on the bleak side, moved their household to Texas when Bose was a tad of five. They settled down west of Fort Worth near the budding town of Weatherford. That was on the very edge of the lands controlled by the Comanches. Ben Ikard had a hankering for the wide-open plains, where he could raise up a herd of horses. Ranching appeared to be a rather simple way of making an honest living for his family. Little did he know that it takes a heap of work to make a ranch run properly. It wasn't too long before he was glad to have his few slaves.

During the years of the War Between the States, there was a great demand for good horseflesh. First it was the Confederacy, then it was the Yankees who needed mounts. Ben considered himself smart, because he had invested most of his money in horses instead of cattle. Trouble was he didn't realize at the time when he was riding the range in search of wild herds that it would take many long, hard hours to break all those mustangs into saddle ponies. When the armies, North and South, placed their orders, they wanted animals that could be ridden by any greenhorn.

A day came when Ben brought in a nice roundup of twenty head. Right away he set to breaking the whole lot of them, but it wasn't too long before they were doing more breaking than he was.

"Why, you old buzzard bait!" swore Ben after being thrown for the third time by the same mare. He pulled himself into a sitting position on the ground and watched the roan buck her way across the corral. He sat there in the dirt, trying to think of an easier way to get the job done properly. He pushed his six-foot frame slowly into a standing position, brushing the dust from his chaps as he did. He sauntered over to the fence where a barefoot Negro boy was perched on the top rail.

It was young Bose. He had been watching his master ride the bucking broncs since finishing most of his chores for the day. He was finding the exhibition to be quite entertaining.

"You get her this time, Massa Ben," said Bose with an ivory grin.

"I don't know, Bose," replied Ben as he leaned against the fence. "I'd give a dollar a horse to any man who could break those broncs for me."

"You can save your money, Massa Ben," said Bose. "I can ride any of them hosses. All I needs is the chance to show you what I can do."

Ben gave Bose a serious eyeballing as he pondered the proposal. He tilted his head one way, then the other. He stroked the stubble of his black beard with a gloved hand and squinted his eyes as he continued to mull over the suggestion.

"You really think you can ride those broncs, boy?" asked Ben.

"Sho'nuff, Massa Ben," answered Bose, showing all his best ivory. "Just give me the chance to do my stuff."

"Okay, boy, I'm going to give you that chance," said Ben. "But go get some boots on first."

Bose was down off the railing and headed for the

shanty that was his family's home before Ben could finish
the order. The boy disappeared inside the rickety shack,
reemerging seconds later. A floppy cloth sombrero was
cockeyed on his head. He struggled with one boot, trying
to get it on one foot as he hopped along on the other. The
hat fell to the ground as he forced the boot over his ankle.
Without losing a single step, he picked up the hat and
raced up to Ben Ikard.

"Don't be in such a hurry, boy," cautioned Ben. "That
mare isn't going anywhere."

"Yessuh, Massa Ben," grinned Bose in his eagerness.

"First get hold of that mare," said Ben, "then we'll see
if you boast idly or if you can ride."

"Yessuh, Massa Ben!" said Bose as he leaped over the
fence and sprinted across the corral to where the horse
was standing. Ben climbed up to where Bose had been
sitting, on the top rail. Knowing that the animal was already a little skittish, Bose stopped plenty short of her.
She swung her head in his direction and snorted a couple
of times. She had had enough trifling for one day, or so
she thought. Bose had other ideas. He stood there, not
more than five agile paces away, his hands on his hips as
he stared the mare right in the eye.

"Now, looky here," said Bose to the horse. "I'm fixin' to
ride you, and I don't want no fussin'." The black youth
tried to look as mean as he could, but that was no easy
trick for him. "You hear me, hoss? I'm gonna ride you,
and you gonna like it."

Bose took one cautious step. The mare held her ground.
She was still snorting and trying to stare down Bose with
her head hung low to the earth, but Bose wasn't buying
her act. He stepped another pace closer. The mare began
to shiver. Another step closer. The mare jerked her head
up as if she was about to bolt.

"Easy, hoss," soothed Bose. "It ain't gonna hurt none. Just you wait and see."

A boy of fourteen, Bose was already the size of a man. In his bare feet, he was near to being six feet tall, but he was still on the skinny side. That made no difference to the mare. All she could see was another human who wanted to get on her back.

Bose was within an arm's length of the reins that touched the dirt beneath the mare's muzzle. Slowly he reached out to grab the leather straps. He had them. The mare shifted her feet, raising her head at the same time. Bose moved in closer, then began stroking her jaw and nose with his free hand.

"See, hoss," whispered Bose, "I ain't gonna do you no harm. All I wants to do is ride you. Now, be a good hoss and let me get right up THERE!"

Just as he was saying the word "there," Bose, quick as lightning, leaped into the saddle. The mare was off guard at first, but she soon recovered her wits, as she began to buck with everything she had left. Bose had a tight hold on the reins as he squeezed his knees into her sides. His boots found the stirrups, and he pushed the soles hard against the steel. The horse twisted and bucked, bucked and twisted, all the time trying to rid herself of one black slave.

Bose had thought bronco busting was easy from where he had sat watching Ben Ikard doing it, but atop that mare he was beginning to find out different. He rolled with every lurch of her back and leaned to the inside when she went into a spin. He felt that her knees were going to buckle at one point. He prepared to eat some corral dust, but the mare maintained her balance.

This went on for what seemed to Bose to be a full ten minutes before the mare finally paid out. Breathing very hard, she came to a standstill, Bose still in the saddle.

"I wouldn't have believed it if I hadn't seen it with my own eyes," said Ben from his perch on the fence rail. "Boy, you *can* ride those broncs. You sure have made me happy. Now I don't have to do it all myself. I can let you take a few turns."

Bose said nothing. He stroked the mare's neck, a smile a prairie wide across his face. He was proud of himself, a good feeling that he wanted always.

Ben cut out another mustang from the herd for Bose to break, and the slave wasted no time getting the job done. He was on his fourth horse when Ben's wife, Arletta, came running from the house.

"Ben Ikard!" she shouted. "What do you think you're doing, letting that boy ride those horses?"

"Bose is a natural bronc buster, Arletta," explained Ben. "Just watch him."

"I don't care, Ben Ikard. You get that boy out of that corral this minute. A young buck like Bose is worth twenty times what a horse is worth."

Ben knew that his wife's words were true, but he realized that they were only true as long as the South continued to fight and slavery remained a way of life in Texas. Unlike many Texans, he was not convinced that the Confederacy would survive the holocaust.

Like most of his neighbors, Ben Ikard did not rush off to join Texas outfits fighting in other parts of the South. He stayed in the state as a Texas Ranger to defend the frontier against marauding Comanches, occasionally coming back to his spread for short visits. He left most of the ranching chores to his slaves. When Ben finally returned home for good, at the conclusion of the war, he found that they had managed the spread almost as well as he could have.

The Texas frontier didn't know the defeat that the rest of the South knew until months after the war was over.

The Unionists and carpetbaggers who filled their land after the cessation of hostilities made it perfectly clear which side had won. As soon as the news of Lee's surrender to Grant circulated throughout the country, all those people who had espoused the Union cause at the outset of the war and who had fled to Kansas or other Union strongholds to be safe from their rebel neighbors in Texas came pouring back to their home state to claim what they had left behind. Northerners and freed slaves, carrying all they possessed in a single satchel, were quick to follow, ready to ravage a defeated people with laws and taxes they would make and twist and have enforced by the victorious occupation armies of the Union. The first duty of the new regime was to ascertain the freedom of all slaves.

"You a free nigger now," said the black man dressed in the finery of a white gentleman. He had collared Bose and a few other young blacks on a street corner of Weatherford. Bose eyed him with suspicion. The man puffed on his cigar. "You can do anythin' you wants to now. You don't have to do nothin' no more for white folks lessen they pays for it. That's the new way. Niggers ain't got to be lickin' the boots of white folks no more. You is free."

Bose wasn't sure what all that meant, but he did know that things weren't going to be the same anymore. He continued to listen to the man with the flowery valise.

"We got rights now. We is gonna be regular citizens, just like the white folks. We can go anyplace we want, and we can do anythin' we want. The law say we can. Why, we can even vote in 'lections."

"'Lections? What's them?" asked one of the listeners.

"'Lections, dummy, is when you gets to have a say in who is gonna be in the go'ment. You make your mark on the paper for the man what you think is the best man for the job. You get to vote for the man of your choice. That's what 'lections is."

Confused, Bose walked away, while the man continued to harangue his gathering.

The streets of Weatherford were a busy place that day. Union soldiers here and there, people going about their regular business in and out of the stores and offices. What disturbed Bose was all the new black faces he was seeing for the first time. They seemed to have sprung from the very earth. Then there were the words of the dude with the cigar. They troubled him even more. He saw Ben Ikard loading some supplies on the buckboard that had brought them into town. Bose approached him about all that was happening too fast for a young man to grasp.

"Massa Ben, that man back there says I is free now," said Bose, motioning behind him with a thumb. "What's he mean by that?"

Ben shook his head, knowing all too well what the man had meant. "Well, Bose, it means that you don't have to call me 'Master Ben' anymore. I am no longer your owner."

"You means you done sold me?" Bose was hurt as well as perplexed.

"No, Bose, I didn't sell you."

Bose's eyebrows narrowed. "Then, who does own me?"

"No one, Bose. From now on, you are your own man. You are no longer a slave."

"I still don't understand, Massa Ben."

"It means that you don't have to work for me if you don't want to. You can go work for any man that will hire you. From the looks of things to come, we'll both be looking for a man to hire us."

Ben was so right. Scalawag judges and shyster lawyers used the courts to take his ranch from him for taxes that were deliberately made so high that hardly any man could pay them. His former slaves would have gladly stayed on with him, even without pay, but when his home was gone, so was theirs. Ben took his family and moved in with friends who managed to keep one step ahead of the tax collectors. Bose went with his parents to live in a little shack on the edge of Weatherford's shantytown. In fact, most of the black people in the area threw up some sort of shelter there. It was the only place for them.

Work was hard to find, especially if you had been a "Johnny Reb" or were black. Most of the ranchers around that part of Texas, the same ones who had offered employment to almost anyone before the war, couldn't afford to pay hired hands. Oliver Loving was an exception, but even so, he could use only a few good men. Ben Ikard was one good man.

The summer days of 1865 were long, dry, and hot on the Texas range. Ben was constantly eating specks of real estate and dodging rattlesnakes as he rounded up the wild longhorns on Loving's spread. The work was too much for the small crew, but Ben made no complaints. He was glad to have a job. He worked hard all through the summer. Then a late-September rain took Ben down with a sickness that forced him to his bed.

"I kind of thought you were pushing yourself harder than the cattle," said Oliver Loving from a chair at Ben's bedside. The cattleman had come by to visit his ailing employee. He was wearing a white duster and still had his gloves on. He held his hat in his hands as he talked. "You were trying to do the work of two men, riding herd on all those beeves. Now I have to find two men to replace you until you are back on your feet."

Ben's fever had broken, but he was a long way from a full recovery. Beads of perspiration blistered on his forehead. When he turned to speak to his boss, some of the sweat rolled off his head onto the pillow and some ran into his eyes.

"Not so, Mr. Loving," Ben got out before a cough interrupted the conversation. Loving wondered if Ben was delirious. "I know a man who could do the job as well, no, better than I have."

"And who might this man be?" asked Loving as he stroked his salt-and-pepper-colored beard.

Ben wiped the salty drops from his eyes, then hacked out his reply. "One of my former slaves."

"A darkie?" Loving had a keen eye, and it stared deep into Ben Ikard. "Can't say that I like the idea of hiring a darkie."

Ikard raised himself up on one elbow. "You want a man who can do the job, don't you, Mr. Loving?"

"Yes, of course. But a darkie?"

Ben knew what he was up against. "This darkie can do the work of two men, and what's more, he'll be happy the whole time he's doing it."

"Who is this boy?"

"His name is Bose. He's living with his folks in Shantytown. You take him on, Mr. Loving, and I'll guarantee you won't be sorry for it."

"I've always trusted you before, Ben Ikard," praised Loving, rising from the chair to his full height of five and a half feet, "and I have no reason to doubt your judgment now. I think I will go see this young buck for myself." He patted Ben's shoulder. "You just get yourself well. I need you on the ranch."

Ben wanted to say farewell, but another bout of coughing permitted him only to wave as Loving left.

The rancher found Bose right where Ben had said he would be. At first sight, Loving wasn't too impressed with him, a gangly boy of eighteen, but on closer inspection his opinion began to change. In the first place, Bose didn't have that musky smell that many Negroes possessed.

"Mr. Ben made me take a bath when I begin to smellin' like a nigger," explained Bose. "Mr. Ben always say that the Comanch' can smell a nigger for miles and miles lessen he takes a bath and gets the smell off hisself."

Loving held the reins of his horse in a hand on his hip. For some reason, he felt that Bose was out of place in Shantytown. The stature of this black youth contrasted against the squalid, ramshackle huts, houses, and lean-tos of the makeshift village. Loving was already beginning to think Ben Ikard would make good on his guarantee.

"Can you ride, boy?" asked Loving.

"Yessuh, I can ride," smiled Bose. "But I ain't got no hoss."

"Can you use a rope?"

Bose was still smiling. "Yessuh. Mr. Ben done learned me to throw a rope."

Loving retrieved a hemp coil from his saddle and handed it to Bose. "Let's just see what you can do with this."

Self-assured, Bose took the line in his left hand. With his right, he quickly and deftly made a loop in it. Then he twirled it over his head, the circle growing with each spin. The lasso flew to its mark, the head of Loving's horse, and with a flick of his wrist, Bose tightened it around the mare's neck.

"That's all very fine," said Loving, not yet convinced, "but can you do it from a galloping horse?"

"Let me get up on that mare, and I'll show you."

Loving nodded his approval, and Bose agilely mounted the animal. He rode off about fifty yards, then came at a gallop toward Loving, all the time swinging the lariat over his head. At the last second, he let the loop fly, encircling Loving with it, and at the same time, he pulled the horse up short of the target. Loving was impressed, because he had hardly felt the rope tighten around him.

"So far," said Loving, disengaging himself from the entangling twine, "you've made me believe that you can do the job, but the only way I will ever know for certain is to take you on."

Bose showed his ivory. "You won't be sorry, Mr. Lovin'."

The cattleman still had two doubts in his mind: his other two hired men. Both were white and had fought for the Confederacy. He wondered how they would feel about working with a colored boy.

Jake Tatum and Frank Willborn had grown up together in various parts of Texas. Their families had come to the then Republic of Texas before they were born. Frank was the older by a year, but Jake was the more outgoing of the pair and thereby the leader. Neither had done too much since leaving the cradle except work hard when it was necessary and play hard when it was convenient. Both had gone through the war unscathed. Both were white and proud of it.

"Boys," said Loving as he introduced his new hand to Jake and Frank in the bunkhouse on his ranch, "this is Bose. He's going to be working with you."

Jake and Frank were sitting at a small table in the middle of the room. They glanced across the array of tin cups and plates, knives, forks, and playing cards on the wooden surface between them. Frank's brow wrinkled, and Jake's face twitched in a slight shrug. Then they turned their attention back to Loving.

"Y'all plannin' on bringin' back slavery, Mr. Lovin'?" asked Jake with a twinkle in his blue eyes and one corner of his mouth crooked in a half smile.

Frank dropped his head and giggled.

Loving was stern. "You can either work with Bose here on my ranch, or you can find a job elsewhere."

"We didn't mean nothin' by it, Mr. Lovin'," Jake groveled, kicking Frank's leg underneath the table at the same time.

"Then, there won't be another occurrence of this sort of thing, will there, Jake?" insisted Loving.

"No, sir," confirmed Tatum.

Loving's eyes shifted to the other man. Frank shook his head sheepishly.

"Good." The rancher glowered back at Jake. "You will see that Bose is settled properly."

"Oh, yes, sir, Mr. Lovin'," agreed Jake.

"Fine. Then, I'll see you boys at sunup," said Loving as he departed.

Bose had stood by during the exchange, sizing up his new co-workers. He was on his own, and he knew it all too well. The thought did not calm him.

"Where do I put my gear?" asked Bose, his voice an octave higher than normal.

Jake hesitated to answer; he wasn't certain yet that Loving was out of earshot. Frank went to a window. When he verified that their employer was on a straight path for the main house, he nodded to Jake.

"Well, now, nigger," began Jake as he slid his chair away from the table, "I'd have y'all sleepin' in the barn with the rest of the animals, but I ain't the boss man around here yet. Mr. Lovin' says y'all get to sleep in here, so y'all just go down there and sleep in the corner. I don't want no musky nigger near me."

Bose chuckled. "Then, I can sleep right here." He put his few belongings on a bunk that was next to Jake's.

Jake jumped up and grabbed a bare black arm. "Didn't y'all hear what I said, boy?"

Ignoring Tatum's hold on him, Bose smiled. "I hear you say you don't want no musky nigger near you. Well, if you takes a good sniff of me, you gonna find that I ain't no musky nigger."

Jake was taken aback. At first he thought the black

youth was being insolent, but the grin on his face gave him reason to doubt that conclusion. Tatum tested the air, and Frank did likewise.

"See?" coaxed Bose. "You don't smell nothin'."

Jake relaxed his grip on Bose's arm. Bose took advantage of it and sat down on the bunk.

"He's right, Jake," said Willborn. "I don't smell a thing."

Jake was still not pleased. "I do." He twitched his nose at the air again, then turned his head toward his lifelong friend. "Somethin' stinks in here." He leaned a little closer toward Frank. "It's you. Y'all stink to high heaven."

"I wouldn't say he was that bad," interjected Bose, "but it's real close. More like hoss apples to me."

Tatum took another whiff. "Yeah, he does smell like a stable floor, don't he, Bose?" Jake broke out laughing. "Why, I blow wind that smells better than he does."

Frank was not too happy about learning of his own odor, but he wasn't too bright either. He simply fell into laughing with Jake.

Bose, seeing that he had changed his adversaries' temperaments, relaxed and joined the merriment.

"Say, Bose," said Frank when his high-pitched giggling subsided. "How come y'all don't stink like most niggers?"

"I takes a bath once a week like Mr. Ben done learned me."

"Ben? Ben Ikard?" quizzed Jake.

"That's right," said Bose. "Mr. Ben was my owner."

"Ben told us about a boy he had," said Jake. "Ben said he was a good ol' boy. Could be he was talkin' about you."

"Mr. Ben coulda been talkin' 'bout my pappy."

"Nope, Ben says he was just a boy," contradicted Jake. He took a good look at Bose. "Well, if Ben Ikard says you're okay, then that's good enough for me. Right, Frank?"

Frank Willborn nodded his approval, and Bose was accepted.

TWO

The winter of 1865–66 was typical of most winters in western Texas. Northers blew cold down from Kansas, occasionally bringing light snow with them. Once in a while, the Gulf of Mexico sent up a warm breeze to take the chill from the air. Then there were times when the two winds would clash over the Plains, the result being a blizzard that was hell on living.

It was late that season when Oliver Loving and his hired hands began to round up his cattle for the summer drive. Loving gathered his three employees in the living room of his house the morning they were to start.

"Frank, you go with me," said the cattleman. "We'll work the south range. Jake, you and Bose take the north. Be sure to take along enough provisions to last you for the week. Take along extra bedrolls. Winter isn't quite through with us yet. Round up twenty or thirty head and bring them back for branding. We'll do it this way for a few weeks or until it looks like we got most of the stock. Be sure not to get anyone else's mixed in with mine. I don't want to cause any hard feelings with my neighbors. Got any questions?"

The three cowboys looked at each other, then back to their employer. Loving had made himself perfectly clear.

"Then, let's get to it," he said, rising from his chair. The cowboys put their hats on and turned to leave. They were almost to the door when Loving spoke again. "Hold on a minute, Bose. I almost forgot something."

They all stopped. Jake and Frank waited at the door while Bose went back toward Loving. He stepped back to the rack of rifles hanging on the wall near the fireplace and over a chest of drawers. Loving opened the top drawer of the oak bureau and removed a pistol. Without closing the drawer, he reached up and took down a rifle. He hefted each weapon, then turned to Bose.

"You might be needing these," said Loving. He pushed a Navy Colt .44 and a Henry repeating rifle toward Bose. "The snakes might be out early, and God only knows what the Kiowas and the Comanches are up to."

Bose made no move to accept the firearms. To give a Negro a gun had always been against the law. Even on the frontier it was an act that just was not done by white folks, but the war had changed all that.

"Go on, take them," insisted Loving. Bose hesitated but did as he was ordered. "You'll be needing cartridges."

Loving returned to the chest to retrieve two boxes of .44 ammunition. He offered them to Bose, whose hands seemed frozen to the Colt and the Henry. He stuffed the revolver in his pants, then reached out for the bullets.

"The long ones are for the rifle," said Loving. "Jake will have to teach you how to handle those guns once you get out on the range." He looked past Bose. "Don't take too long to do it, Jake. You don't know how soon you'll be needing his gun hand."

"Yes, sir, Mr. Lovin'," obeyed Jake. "I'll get to teachin' him right off. Y'all so right about them Kiowas and Comanches. They could be anywheres."

"Well, enough said," commented Loving. "Let's be getting to work."

Loving picked up his hat from the desk and headed for the door. Jake opened it for everyone. Frank followed his boss outside. Bose didn't budge. He was transfixed by the shooting irons.

"Come on, Bose," called Jake. "There's work to be done." Bose was silent, not moving. "Bose! Let's get!"

Tatum's shouted command awakened the youth to action. "Sure thing, Jake." He shoved the .44 shells in his coat pockets and made for the door.

Within the hour, the two pairs of men were riding in opposite directions across the prairie in search of stray cattle. The Loving ranch didn't encompass too many square miles, as far as Texas cattle ranches went. If it had been fenced in, the problem of rounding up the stock would have been minimal. There was the rub: barbed wire had yet to find its place on the open plains. Cattle were free to roam as much as the buffalo. A man's herd could wander a hundred miles away over a long winter.

Jake and Bose rode in silence the first hour they were out. Each led an extra mount loaded with their supplies. Once they found some strays they would make a camp and begin herding the longhorns. Until then, they would drift along with nothing more to do than talk.

"Why do y'all reckon Mr. Lovin' put us together, Bose?" asked Jake as he started the conversation.

"Don't know," replied Bose.

"I would've thought he'd put me and Frank together, seein' as how we're always together anyway. Why didn't he take me with him instead of Frank? For that matter, why didn't he take you? He's always sayin' what a good ol' boy y'all are. Nope, can't figure this out. What y'all make of it, Bose?"

"Don't make nothin' of it," answered Bose. "The man say go one way, I go. I don't ask no questions. I figure the man pays me the money, and that give him the right to tell me what to do and when to do it. That's all I know."

Jake shook his head. "I should've known not to ask a dumb nigger what was on his mind. Hell, Bose, y'all as dumb as dirt. Hmph! And to think that Mr. Lovin' wants me to teach you how to shoot. What does he think I am? Your nigger mammy or somethin'?"

"Hold on, Jake," Bose interrupted. "I know why Mr. Lovin' done sent me out with you."

"Oh, you figured that out, huh? Well, y'all just tell me why he sent us out together."

"It's 'cause you talk too much," smiled Bose.

"I what? Talk too much? Well, will y'all listen to that? An uppity nigger tellin' me I talk too much. Nigger, y'all lucky you get to sleep in the same room with white folks."

"And next to one too," laughed Bose.

"I should've known. I should've known that the minute I let you sleep in the bunk next to mine y'all'd never let me live it down."

Bose broke out with a long chuckle. "You should consider it a privilege to have a clean nigger like me sleepin' in the next bunk. If you don't stop that snorin' at night, I'm gonna quit takin' a bath ev'ry Saturday. Then what are you gonna do?"

"Then I'm gonna shoot me a musky nigger." Jake patted the six-gun at his side, then laughed raucously. "Speakin' of shootin', maybe we'd better have that first lesson right now."

"I don't know about that, Jake," argued Bose, the smile gone from his face.

Over the months, Jake had come to know Bose quite well, or at least he thought he had. Bose's reluctance to learn the use of firearms was something that he couldn't understand. Even though his friend was black, he was still young, and most men his age couldn't wait for a chance to prove their skill with a handgun. No, thought Jake, something was troubling this colored boy.

"Now, why don't y'all know about that?" quizzed Tatum.

"I just don't, that's all," Bose replied as if he was trying to avoid the topic altogether.

"Y'all ain't afraid, are yuh, Bose?"

Bose jerked his head sideways. "What do you mean, 'afraid'? I ain't afraid of nothin'. You know that, Jake."

"Then, why won't you try to learn how to shoot?"

No answer came from Bose.

"There ain't nothin' to it." Jake drew his Colt from its holster. "Y'all just aim it like this and squeeze the trigger real gentle and . . ." The gun fired off a round. ". . . and y'all shoot whatever y'all are aimin' to shoot."

"What if it was a man at the end of that barrel? What then, Jake?"

"Now, that all depends," said Jake, slower than usual. "If it was a white man, y'all would be in a heap of trouble. If it was another nigger, I don't think anyone would pay too much mind to it. If it was a redskin, folks would be thinkin' up ways to praise you for your good deed."

It wasn't all that simple, and Bose knew it. An untamed land had its advantages for a black man, but it also had some of the drawbacks of more civilized areas, even if not as pronounced. Carrying a gun was a great responsibility, mostly because it invited others who were also heeled to throw down on you. Bose knew that all too well. He had heard how a boy named John Hardin had shot and killed a Negro just because he was toting a weapon. Bose didn't want any son of a rebel taking aim at him just because he was armed. "Well, maybe so," said Bose, "but couldn't you wait to learn me, Jake?"

"Nope. There ain't no time like the present, as the sayin' goes. Get down off that horse, and let's commence to learnin' you how to shoot."

Bose knew that further argument was useless. Jake wasn't about to take any more negative responses. He alit from his horse, as did Jake from his.

"Let me see that piece Mr. Lovin' gave you," said Jake.
Bose handed him the pistol. "Not the best shootin' iron
there is, but it'll kill Comanches and rattlesnakes." He
aimed the gun into the distance and pulled the trigger.
The only sound coming forth was an empty click. "Why,
you ain't even got it loaded."

"I don't know how," apologized Bose.

"Well, looky close here, Bose, 'cause I'm about to show
y'all how to do it." Jake took five cartridges from the box
that Loving had given Bose. "Now, y'all only put five
shells in, 'cause when you're carryin' this thing you want
to keep it on an empty chamber. If you keep it on a
loaded chamber, it might go off and shoot you in the foot
or leg or somewheres worse." He inserted the bullets one
by one. "There now, it's loaded." He gave the gun back to
Bose, who balked at taking it. "Go ahead and take it,
Bose. It won't hurt you as long as you treat it with respect."

The day wasn't hot, but you couldn't tell it by the way
Bose was sweated up. He reached out with one shaky
hand to receive the six-shooter. His slippery palm almost
dropped the piece. His eyes, normally round and full of
joy, were as big as two fried eggs with burned yolks.

"Take it easy, pard," soothed Jake. "Get a good grip on
the handle. Now pull the hammer back till it locks."

His thumb slipped off the hammer on the first try, but
fortunately it was on an empty chamber. He succeeded in
getting the hammer in its proper position on the second
attempt. Then, without thinking, he pulled the trigger.
The noise scared both men, but Jake was especially
frightened when the bullet spewed up dust between his
feet. He jumped away as if to seek cover, but there was
none to be had.

"Lordy, nigger!" Jake shouted. "You crazed in the head
or somethin'? What are you tryin' to do? Shoot my toes off

or somethin'? Give me that thing!" He grabbed the gun away from Bose.

"I'm sorry, Jake," Bose pleaded. "I didn't mean to make it go off like that. I'm real sorry."

Tatum looked at his rattled friend. "Now, take it easy, Bose. No harm done. I know y'all didn't mean to shoot the dad-blamed thing." He returned the Colt to Bose. "Now, this time keep your finger off the trigger when y'all go to cock it." Then he added, "And point it the other way."

Bose did better this time. He pulled the hammer back, locking it in place, then took careful aim away from Jake and the horses before squeezing off a round. The explosion jumped his arm back, but the noise bothered him more.

"Now, look here, Bose. When you shoot this thing for real, y'all got to forget about the bang. Just concentrate on what you're shootin' at. That's the important thing to remember. It's the target that counts, 'specially if it's a Comanche who wants to kill you first or if it's a rattlesnake. With a rattlesnake, you only get one chance before he strikes. You might get two chances with a Comanche, but he surely won't give a third. Now fire off those other three bullets as fast as you can, then load up again."

Bose shot off the remaining shells and reloaded the .44 just as Jake had shown him. "Now what?" he asked.

"Now put that piece away and get back on your horse. That's enough gun-learnin' for now. I'll learn y'all how to use that Henry later."

Jake didn't get around to teaching Bose the rudiments of shooting a rifle until they were back at the ranch the following week. The primary purpose for them to be out on the range interfered with any more lessons.

Loving had told the two cowboys that they were to stay out for a week gathering in strays. Six of those seven

days passed, and Jake and Bose had rounded up over fifty
cows, steers, and bulls; calves didn't count. They bedded
them down for the last night before heading back. Bose
took the first watch as Jake laid out his bedroll.

Bose let his horse graze around the perimeter of the
herd. Occasionally, he would look up at the heavens.
They had always fascinated him. Although he had no ed-
ucation in astronomy, he knew that certain stars appeared
each night in the same patterns and in the same approxi-
mate locations. He taught himself to tell time by the con-
stellations in relationship between their heavenly position
and the horizon. He knew that he was only halfway
through his watch when the wind began to pick up in velocity and a cloud cover rolled in. He also took note of the
cattle, many of which had taken to their feet. When they
started to meander in the same direction that the grass
was bending, he knew that it was a bad sign. He decided
to awaken Jake.

"The herd's movin'," said Bose as he nudged Jake with
one foot. "Get yourself up, boy. We got trouble."

"Who y'all callin' a boy, nigger?" growled Jake.

"Never mind that now, Jake. We got to be movin' too,
or we're gonna have cows all over the place again."

Without waiting to be told a second time, Jake was on
his feet and into his boots. He wadded up his bedroll as
Bose brought his horse, already saddled, to him. They
loaded up the other two mounts with their gear and supplies as they broke camp. Each man took a packhorse as
they rode off to opposite flanks of the herd.

The longhorns weren't stampeding, and they didn't
seem inclined to be in any distress. Like all cattle in a
winter storm, they turned their tails to the wind to move
with it. Jake and Bose knew that they would react this
way as they tried to keep track of the herd until sunrise,

all the time hoping that with the coming of daylight they could point them in a desired direction.

The norther blew with greater intensity, and then the worst happened: it began to snow.

Throughout the night, the two cowboys let the cattle have their way. Riding here and there, they only tried to keep them bunched up. The going was slow, and as the snow accumulated across the prairie, it became even slower. Partly because of the blinding snow and partly because of the heavy overcast, visibility improved very little with the new day.

"This ain't good," hollered Jake over the wind. "I can't tell where we are now, and I ain't even sure which way we're goin'."

"South," Bose yelled back. "We're headin' south."

Jake didn't know how Bose figured that, but he was willing to take his word for it. "Well, I s'pose we'll just have to keep movin' with them."

"Not for much longer, Jake. There's an arroyo just up ahead a piece. If we can get the cattle into it, we can hole up there till the storm blows itself out."

Jake rode back to his spot on the far side of the herd, baffled by Bose's reckoning. He told himself that he would have to ask Bose about it when they were settled in someplace.

As Bose had said, an arroyo was just ahead of them. The edge of it in front of them dropped off two or three feet; it was hard to tell with all the snow covering it. The opposite side was a snowbank drifted high by the wind. The longhorns balked at going into the ravine, but a little prodding by the cowboys got the leaders to take the drop, the rest following without hesitation. Some of the cattle stumbled and tumbled in the snow, but they were soon back on their feet, bawling the whole time.

"We got to head this way," Bose shouted through his

bandana, motioning with his free hand at the same time. "There's a bunch of trees down that way a piece."

All the cattle were into the wash. Jake rode back and forth at one side of the herd, forcing them to walk in the direction Bose had indicated. Bose worked on pointing the leaders. Some longhorns tried climbing the far bank, but it did little good, as the snow was too deep for them. One by one, they realized that the cowboys had the right idea.

The wind was hardly noticeable down in the arroyo. The cattle didn't seem as anxious as when they were on the plain, and the cowboys were glad to get that icy breath off their necks.

A clump of cottonwoods was there, just as Bose had said it would be. They weren't very tall trees, and with the bushes around them, they offered good protection for the herd from the storm. Snow was drifted against the shrubbery, offering more shelter from the wind. The cowboys drove the cattle into the center of the copse, which formed a natural corral with two "gates." Jake stood watch at one, and Bose sat upon his horse at the other. The herd settled down to wait out the tempest around them.

The snow stopped falling before dark closed in, but the wind continued its howl long into the night. All the time, Jake and Bose kept to their posts, neither taking leave for any reason. The longhorns milled around inside the thicket, pounding down the snow enough to uncover some grass. When they weren't digging their muzzles through the cold wet for food, they huddled close together for warmth. The cowboys didn't have that luxury.

The next morning dawned clear and bright, but the wind was still a constant companion to Bose and Jake. The sun tried its best to warm things a bit, but the norther kept the air as icy as before. Bose rode back up to where Jake had stationed himself to find his friend asleep in the saddle. A snort from Bose's horse awakened him.

"Jake, it ain't gonna do us no good to wait no more. This here arroyo runs down to the river, the same river that runs by the ranch. We can take the cattle down there, but if we do, they might scatter. If we stay here, we gonna freeze for sure."

Jake mulled over their options through the weariness of his mind. "Well, freezin' ain't my way of dyin'. I guess we'll have to take our chances at the river."

They got the cattle moving again, heading them south. The herd was strung out up and down the ravine, no more than two abreast at any one place until the arroyo widened near the river valley. At that point, Jake moved the stragglers closer to the leaders, which Bose was doing his best to slow down. The river was low but running crystal clear. The beasts waded into the stream to drink, and Jake and Bose permitted their mounts the same privilege. The water ran to the southeast, as most waterways in Texas do. Both cowboys knew they could follow it back to safety and comfort that very day if they abandoned the cattle. That was the catch to it: they had spent too many days rounding up the animals to let them scatter again. Safety and comfort would have to wait.

The wind, although shifting toward the east, eased off by midday, and the sun fought even harder to warm the air. The herd appeared less anxious over their fate than before, and Jake felt it was a time to relax their vigilance. Bose had other ideas.

"We're still a long way from the ranch," said Bose. "The storm done drove the cows in the wrong direction. We got to move 'em back the other way now."

"But that's into the wind, Bose," argued Jake.

"That's gonna make it all the harder," said Bose, "but that's the direction of the ranch."

"Then I suppose we best get to it." Jake sighed, because he had reservations about the task ahead. He knew all too well that the chances of the cattle scattering on them would be increased by turning them into the wind. "Come on, hoss; we got us a job to do."

The cattle didn't like the idea of walking into the breeze. Some bolted from the herd, while others simply stood their ground, stubbornly refusing to move.

"H-yah! H-yah!" the cowboys shouted. Each man rode around the herd, digging spurs into the flanks of their mounts. The horses responded, almost knowing exactly what was being demanded of them before their riders demanded it: in and out, cutting here, dodging there. Man and horse were as one being, trying to maintain the cows, calves, bulls, and steers as a herd. There was no time to think, to calculate a move. Only reflex counted. And finally the cattle accepted the guidance of the two men on horseback. Into the wind they went.

At sundown, the wester settled to a soft whistle, and the ever-present cold reached down inside both men at their very bones. The herd was halted on the prairie for what Jake thought would be until sunrise.

"Jake, we might well keep 'em movin' through the night," said Bose as he brought his horse alongside Jake's. "The cows still seem to be too restless to stay together."

"How are we gonna find the ranch in the dark, you dumb nigger?"

"All we got to do is watch the stars," Bose smiled. "They're clear and bright tonight. We can use them to guide us home."

Jake had his doubts, but he had gone along with Bose on everything so far. There was no reason to start being too contrary.

"You take the lead, then," said Jake, "but if you're just

bein' a smart-alecky nigger on me, you're gonna pay for it. You hear me, Bose."

"I hear you," Bose laughed, then rode off to get the herd moving again.

Jake kicked his horse into action, and the cattle bawled their approval. They didn't know where they were being driven to, but they were satisfied to be going somewhere. They walked steadily through the night.

The morning sun proved Bose to be right. The ranch buildings were silhouetted against the rainbow colors of the sunrise. The windows were all dark, and just wisps of smoke came from the chimneys of the main house and the bunkhouse. It was evident that people were there, but they had yet to awaken.

"Well, I'll be," swore Jake when he saw the ranch straight ahead of them. "That is one smart nigger."

Oliver Loving kept forty acres fenced in near the ranch houses. It was a good place to hold the range stock before branding time. Bose pointed the longhorns in its direction, but before the herd could reach the entrance, the ranch was astir. Loving was the first to greet Bose as he was about to open the gate.

"Got caught in the storm, did you?" queried Loving.

"That's right," said Jake as he rode up. "We'd still be out there if it wasn't for Bose here."

"Is that a fact?" Loving squinted at Jake, then he realized that he shouldn't have asked.

"Yessir, Mr. Lovin', it sure is," began Jake. "Why, Bose here is a reg'lar compass. Why, he. . . ."

Jake went on and on, recounting how Bose had saved him and the cattle from certain death. Bose simply went about his job.

THREE

"Which trail you plannin' to take, Mr. Lovin'?" asked Bose as he sat atop his horse.

Oliver Loving looked over the thousand head that his hands had rounded up that spring. "I don't know yet, Bose. The Missouri border gangs are causing more trouble than ever, I hear. The Comanches and Kiowas are just as troublesome the other way. I'm not certain that we have enough men to ward off a raid by either the Indians or the border gangs."

"Maybe there's another way we can go," offered Bose.

Loving shook his head as he reined his horse away from the herd. "If there is, I'll gladly take it." He rode back to the cabin that he used as an office during branding.

Loving didn't know that a younger cowman was about to change his life. He was tall and lean as he sat straight in the saddle. Loving didn't know him by sight, but he had heard some fairly straight stories about this man of Texas. Charles Goodnight, twenty years younger than Loving, rode into the Loving camp.

"Getting ready for a drive?" Goodnight asked the first cowboy he approached.

"Yep," came the terse reply.

"Who's heading up this outfit?" asked Goodnight.

"Mr. Loving."

"Mr. Oliver Loving?" The cowboy nodded. Goodnight knew of the man. He scratched at his unshaven face. "Where might I find Mr. Loving?"

The cowboy saved his words again. His hat nodded toward a shack where Goodnight could see a middle-aged man hunched over some papers on a small table in front of the building.

"Much obliged, friend," said Goodnight as he kicked his horse toward the shack. He halted the animal at a hitching rail and then dismounted, knowing that Loving was watching him. Goodnight was intentionally sure as he tied the reins to the rail. Then he added deliberation to his stride as he stepped over to the table.

"Mr. Loving?"

"I am the same," replied Loving.

"I am Charles Goodnight. I am honored to make your acquaintance, sir."

Hands were extended in greeting.

"The honor is mine, Mr. Goodnight. I have heard many great things of you."

"And I of you, sir." Goodnight smiled warmly. "I see that you are preparing for a drive."

"No, I am all prepared," contradicted Loving. "I am delayed by my own indecision. I am in a tight about which trail to take."

A ripple of excitement coursed through Goodnight, but he fought back the emotion. "I am also going on a drive. I am just now returning to my herd to begin." He paused as caution dictated his words. "I have been to Fort Worth, where I secured the legal powers to dispose of the cattle in my herd which are not mine."

Loving knew that Goodnight had a reputation for being trustworthy. "Which trail will you be taking? The east or the west?"

"Neither, sir. I plan to strike out for Colorado."

"But that will take you through Comanche country."

"Not by the trail I propose to take, Mr. Loving." Goodnight was certain that the older man's interest was had with those words.

"Please, Mr. Goodnight, won't you join me inside? I have a bottle of fine sipping whiskey there." Loving rose from his chair and led the way. "I keep it hidden there from my hands. I do not imbibe to any excess myself, but I do like the feel of good liquor on my palate."

"As do I," said Goodnight as he entered the shack with Loving. He watched the older man step over to the fireplace, where he removed a large stone from the foot of the hearth. Almost magically, Loving produced the bottle of spirits. He offered the container to Goodnight for his examination, while he retrieved two tin cups from a rack on the wall.

"If you would do the honors, Mr. Goodnight," said Loving as he held out the two cups. The younger man poured two fingers full into each cup, then placed the flask on the table next to them. Loving handed one cup over to his guest. "To your health, sir."

"And to yours, sir," toasted Goodnight before drinking.

With the fire of the whiskey still coursing its way to his stomach, Loving renewed the conversation. "Please, Mr. Goodnight, tell me of this trail that you plan to take to Colorado. I am much interested in entering that market myself."

"It is not a new route as such, Mr. Loving," began Goodnight, "but I believe that it has yet to be traveled by cattlemen. The route of the Overland Stage travels to the southwest from this region. It is a well-worn trail all the way to the Pecos. There is plenty of grass along the way, and there is also water. That is all true except for the last hundred miles to the river. In that stretch lies the danger. It is desert."

"A hundred miles is a long way to drive cattle without

water," commented Loving. "How do you propose to overcome this hazard?"

"At the last water hole," Goodnight continued, "the herd will be rested and allowed to drink to their fill. Then we will begin to drive them late in the day, when the sun is not so hot. We will continue into the night, then rest them until early morning. The drive will continue until the sun is high, and then we will stop until late afternoon, when we continue again as before."

"That sounds reasonable," said Loving.

"Once we reach the river," Goodnight went on, "it will be only a matter of driving the cattle up the Pecos Valley to Fort Sumner and Bosque Redondo. I hear that the Army is in dire need of beeves for the Navajos. What we cannot sell there, we will drive over the mountains to Colorado. I am told that the mining camps will pay almost any price for good beef."

Loving was thoughtful. "You are determined to attempt this route?"

"I am," Goodnight said firmly.

"Then, if you will let me, I will go with you."

Goodnight was delighted. "I will not only let you, but it is the most desirable thing of my life. I not only need the assistance of your force, but I need your advice."

"Then, it is settled," said Loving. "When do we leave?"

"As soon as we can join herds," said Goodnight. "Mine is ready to move."

"And mine," said Loving. "Shall we meet at Belknap, say the day after tomorrow?"

"That does me fine," smiled Goodnight.

"To the sixth and on to Colorado," said Loving as he lifted his cup in the air.

Goodnight did likewise. "On to Colorado."

Both men swallowed hard on the whiskey. Loving put his cup down on the table, then hurried over to the door.

Goodnight followed him outside. Bose Ikard was just then riding up to the corral to draw a new horse from Loving's remuda. Goodnight saw the black cowboy and was taken aback. He tapped Loving on the shoulder before the older man could call out to Bose.

"You employ niggers, Mr. Loving?" Goodnight frowned.

Loving understood Goodnight's question and all its implications. He had been a Unionist during the recent conflict, whereas Goodnight had served the South in the Texas Rangers.

Loving turned to confront his guest. "Yes, I do, Mr. Goodnight. But I do not hire just any colored boy who comes along. This man has been with me since last year, and he is worth every dollar that I pay him. He knows his job as well as any man I have."

Goodnight was not appeased. "It is not to my liking, Mr. Loving, to have a nigger on this drive."

"Is the objection solely yours, sir?" Loving was becoming indignant.

"No, sir. I do not judge a man by his color. I am just thinking of the men in my own employ. 'Most all fought for the South."

"The war is over, Mr. Goodnight," Loving interrupted, "and the sooner that all learn that, the better all will be."

"I concur, Mr. Loving." Goodnight backed off, knowing that he was not about to sway Loving's mind.

"Besides Bose there, I have three other coloreds in my employ, all of whom shall accompany us on this drive."

Goodnight was astounded. One black cowboy was already too many for him, but four was out of the question. He started to argue the point further, but then his own words came back to him about how he needed Loving for his advice as well as his force. Goodnight swallowed his prejudice for the moment.

"If you say so, Mr. Loving. I shall repair to Weatherford for supplies, then meet you at Belknap on the sixth. Good day, sir."

Loving acknowledged the farewell and watched Goodnight mount up and ride off. With his new partner out of sight, he returned to the business at hand.

"Bose, come here," he shouted across the yard. Bose looked toward his employer. "I have good news."

"Good news," said Bose as he strode up to Loving. "That's what I like to hear."

"Tell everyone that we shall be moving the herd first thing tomorrow," said Loving.

"That is good news," smiled Bose. "Which trail you done decided to take?"

"Neither," toyed Loving. "We shall be striking a new trail with Mr. Goodnight, the man who was just here." He motioned toward the horizon, where a cloud of dust was being thrown up by Goodnight's horse. "We shall join our herd with his the day after tomorrow at Belknap, and then we shall strike out for Colorado."

"Colorado?" quizzed Bose. "Where's that place?"

"North and west of here." Loving studied the worried look on Bose's face. "Don't let it bother you, Bose. It's a long way from Texas, and it's going to be a long trail and a great deal of work all the way."

"Yessir, Mr. Lovin', if you say so." Bose turned away, then back to Loving. "Colorado?"

"That's right," his boss smiled. "Colorado."

Bose started to walk away again. He considered asking Loving one more time, but then thought better of it. He didn't know this place, and it troubled him. Just how big the world was he would never know. He walked slowly back to the corral for his horse.

Jake and Frank were sitting on the corral fence, watching Tom Brannon catch fresh mounts for them and Bose.

Jake's head inclined to see Bose returning from talking with their employer.

"Hey, Bose," cried Jake. "What did the ol' man say?"

Bose didn't answer immediately but kept walking toward them. He climbed up the rails and perched himself next to Jake. The two white cowboys waited patiently for his reply.

"Jake, where is Colorado?" asked Bose.

Frank nudged Jake, then said, "Mr. Lovin' said we was goin' to Colorado?"

"Is that what he said, Bose?" asked Jake.

"That's what he said," answered Bose, "but what I want to know is where is Colorado?"

Jake and Frank exchanged glances, each wondering if Bose was pulling a joke on them.

"Are y'all sure he said Colorado?" asked Jake as he concentrated on Bose.

"I done said that's what he said," complained Bose. "Now tell me about this here Colorado."

"It's a far piece from here," said Jake. "It's got lots of purty mountains with lots of purty gold in them."

"Yeah, but how do we get there?" queried Bose.

"The only way I know is across Comanche country," offered Frank. "That don't seem right, though. I can't imagine Mr. Lovin' wantin' to go through Comanche country."

"Me neither," said Jake.

Bose was silent. The name "Comanche" didn't set too well on his ears. Whenever he heard the word, he was reminded of a horrible experience. It had happened that same spring.

Bose was out rounding up more steers and cows for the upcoming drive. Jake and Frank were working with him. The three of them had nearly a hundred head in their herd and were preparing to return to the ranch when they

came across the most terrifying sight that Bose had ever
seen.

Frank was the first to notice the vultures circling in the
air. Their presence could mean only one thing: something
was dying or was dead on the prairie ahead of them. Jake,
then Bose, noticed the buzzards, and all three men left
the cattle to see what the birds' prey might be. They
halted their horses just short of it.

"Who y'all think they were?" asked Frank.

"Don't know," said Jake. "Probably just a couple of
cowpokes chasin' down steers, like us."

Bose was quiet as he looked down on the remains of
two white men staked out on the ground. Both had been
stripped naked, exposing their wounds. One had a hole in
his right shoulder and one in his left thigh. The other had
been shot with an arrow through his left side. Their scalps
were gone, and their feet were charred. Their tormentors
had evidently had their fun before they died.

"Poor devils," said Frank.

"Yeah, well, we better bury them," said Jake. "Can't
leave them for the buzzards."

Jake and Frank dismounted, but Bose sat still, his gaze
transfixed on the two corpses.

Jake looked up at Bose's bulging eyes. "First time y'all
seen somethin' like this, Bose?"

Bose swallowed hard. "I ain't never seen nothin' like
this before. Who done this terrible thing?"

"Comanches, most likely," said Jake. "Maybe Kiowas.
One thing for sure: it was Injuns. Come on, now, and
help us bury these poor souls."

Frank had already cut the rawhide bindings that held
the victims' arms and legs to the stakes. Jake found three
sharp stones, and they went to scraping at the rock-hard
soil of the prairie. It took them nearly an hour to make
two holes deep enough to cover the bodies. They laid the

two men to rest, and Jake said a few Christian words over their graves.

"Well, let's get on back," said Jake at the end of the ceremony. "We got a herd to move."

The three men mounted their horses and started back to the cattle that remained grazing where the cowboys had left them. Before they could get too far, Bose noticed something move on the rise to the north of them.

"Jake, what do you make of that up there?" he asked.

Jake and Frank turned to see Bose pointing a finger toward the horizon. "Can't tell. What y'all make of it, Frank?"

"Looks like riders to me," said Frank. Then he put a squint to his eyes. "Good God Almighty! It's Injuns!"

"Jesus Christ, it is!" exclaimed Jake. "Let's run for it."

"But the cattle," said Bose as Jake and Frank put spurs to their mounts.

"To hell with the cattle!" shouted Jake over his shoulder. "Let the Injuns have them."

Bose looked at the Indians coming down the hill at a gallop, then at his two fleeing friends. Slowly, he took his Henry rifle from its scabbard.

"Mr. Lovin' wants them cattle," he said to himself, "and no Injun's gonna get them."

He took careful aim and cut loose a round. The Indians, at least twenty of them, kept coming. He looked down the sights of the rifle again, then squeezed off another shot. Still they came on, closing to within two hundred yards. His third bullet finally found a mark. One Comanche flipped backward from his pony.

Frank and Jake heard the shooting and looked back to see Bose atop his horse, firing away at the attackers. Then the two cowboys looked at each other.

"Aw, heck," said Jake. "That dumb nigger is gonna get himself killed."

"It does look that way," said Frank.

Both men shrugged and pulled their horses up short.

"We just can't let him get killed all by himself," said Jake.

"Maybe someone'll come along and bury us, too," said Frank. He reached for his rifle, as did Jake. "I'm with you, pard."

They turned and raced back to where Bose was holding his ground. He had dismounted and was keeping a steady fire going at the Comanches. Two of them lay on the prairie, having taken lead from the Henry, but there were still plenty of Indians coming his way. They had spread out and seemed to be attacking him from all directions at once. He drew a bead on the one he thought had the most feathers in his war bonnet. The rifle cracked, and the chief reeled back, then forward as he tried desperately to remain on his horse. With their leader wounded, the others slowed the assault. The Comanches were less than fifty yards away when Jake and Frank joined in the fight.

"Dumb nigger!" shouted Jake. "Y'all tryin' to get us all killed?"

Bose didn't answer. Instead, he pulled off another round, and another brave plunged from his horse. Jake and Frank jumped to the ground, rifles in hand. Whereas Bose had taken careful aim with each shot, they simply started shooting in the general direction of their adversaries. The Comanches had yet to get off a single arrow or bullet at them. When two more warriors were knocked from their ponies, the rest scattered, picking up their dead and wounded as they retreated over the hill.

Jake gave them a hard look. "They're runnin' now, but they'll be back. Y'all can bet on that."

"Yeah," Frank agreed, "so let's get out of here."

"Not without Mr. Lovin's cattle," said Bose.

"To hell with them cows," said Jake. "My hair's worth

a lot more to me than them mangy critters. Let's get the hell out of here."

"Not without the cattle," Bose said adamantly.

Jake scanned the prairie, then turned to Bose. "Look here, Bose. The herd is scattered all over tarnation. It'll take us half a day to get them back together again."

"Then, we best get to it," he said as he mounted his horse.

"Y'all are the stubbornest nigger I ever did see," said Jake as he also mounted up. "Come on, Frank. We might as well help this dumb nigger round up them beeves."

Frank climbed onto his steed, and the cowboys went about their business, all the while watching for signs of a renewed attack by the Comanches. The herd was together again in a few hours, and the drive continued as before. Jake and Frank rode high flank, one to each side of the cattle, and Bose brought up the rear.

"I can see it happenin' again," said Frank to himself. "Them Comanches will be comin' back here again, and this time they're gonna get my hair for sure. All because of one stubborn nigger."

Frank was wrong. The Comanches were finished for that day. Bose had killed their war chief, and they had gone to celebrate his death. The drovers and their cattle were safe.

FOUR

The Loving and the Goodnight herds were joined twenty-five miles southwest of Belknap on the prescribed date. Together they had over two thousand head of mixed cattle and a force of eighteen well-armed men, not including the cook and themselves. The two partners considered this to be a sufficient number to ward off any attacks, whether they came from Comanches, Kiowas, or the Apaches they might encounter once they entered New Mexico. Indian forays were not their major concern. It was their feeling that the desert would be the greatest enemy to overcome.

The first few days on the trail were routine. Goodnight gave over the reins of leadership to Loving, more because he wanted to spend his time scouting than in deference to Loving's age or experience. The older partner confined his activities to riding herd on the drovers.

Nearly every daylight hour would see Loving ride the full length of the herd. He would start from the chuck wagon early in the morning and ride to the point, where one man was stationed on each side of the leaders. Gradually, he would drift back along the windward side, checking the five men on that flank. As he reached the tail of the drifting mass of beeves, he would stop to see how things were going with the four cowboys riding drag. Then he would drop back even farther to visit with the two men driving the remuda. From there, he would pass a few more words with the drag men before riding up the

leeward side. Those five cowboys were always glad to
have him come by, because it would give them a few moments to turn their backs on the gigantic dust cloud that
the cattle raised each day. On every other trip around,
Loving would encounter Goodnight returning to the
chuck wagon from a scouting sortie. The younger man
would pass on any pertinent information about the trail
ahead, and Loving would then repeat it to the cowboys.

The herd traveled without incident into the wilderness,
which had seen few white men and even fewer longhorns.
The outfit passed Camp Cooper and then drove past Fort
Phantom Hill. Mile after mile eating dust, they continued
through Buffalo Gap. The drive went by Fort Chad-
bourne, moving south and west. They crossed the North
Concho River, then made for the Middle Concho, which
they followed for twenty miles before finding a suitable
ford for crossing. There they remained for two days, re-
cruiting the herd and resting their horses for the trial of
the desert ahead.

The cook had his fires going and a hot meal of beef and
beans cooking when the weary cowboys finished bedding
down the cattle for the night. Those who were not left to
stand the first watch gathered around the chuck wagon
with their eating utensils at the ready. Loving and Goodnight stood some distance away, tin cups of hot coffee in
hand as they discussed the day past and the days ahead.
As was their custom, they would eat last.

"We will let the cattle rest here," said Goodnight as he
warmed his hands around the metal cup. "The desert is
directly in front of us."

"I'll have the boys bring the herd as close to the river
as possible," said Loving. "The cattle can drink to their
fill, and we can head them out late in the afternoon tomorrow."

"I was thinking that we should wait an additional day,"

offered Goodnight. "That will give the men time to rest
for the days ahead."

"A wise decision," concurred Loving. He looked over at
the four black cowboys that he had brought along. A
thought amused him, so he shared it with his partner. "I
was just wondering, Charlie, if you have changed your
opinion about my coloreds."

Goodnight smiled as he also looked at the four men. "It
was not my opinion in the first place, Oliver, but now that
you bring up the subject I must say that I am somewhat
impressed by their abilities to do the job. I have not heard
any grumbling among my men about working with
niggers. The reason for that could be that I instructed
them that there would be no such talk permitted. If any
one of them didn't like working with niggers, he could
collect his pay and find employment elsewhere."

Loving nodded his approval. "I'm glad to hear you talk
like that, Charlie. Those boys have always given me an
honest day's work, especially Bose there. He was the first
colored that I hired. Ben Ikard, God rest his soul, his former owner, recommended him to me. I must confess that
I, too, had my doubts at first, but after having Bose work
for me for a few days, I came to a different opinion. He
has yet to make me regret for one moment my hiring
him."

"He appears to be a leader among the niggers," said
Goodnight.

"Yes, the others do seem to follow his lead. I see that as
a good sign. Bose leads by his example, not words. Even
some of my white drovers follow his example. I have
often thought of making him my foreman."

"Why haven't you?" asked Goodnight.

"Because he is so young. The boy is only nineteen, or
so he tells me. I sometimes think he is older. His actions
seem to make him so."

Just at that time, Jim Fowler was speaking to Bose
about a particular problem he was having. Jim, who was
also a former slave and three years older than Bose, had
been riding drag each day, and he was having trouble
keeping the cows with new calves moving along with the
herd.

"What I gonna do about that, Bose?" asked Jim.

"Don't know, Jim," replied Bose as he wiped away the
last bit of grease from his meal. "You best ask Mr. Lovin'
about that."

"I get all twisted up in my mouth when I got to talk
with the man," alibied Jim.

"Then, you come with me," said Bose as he put down
his plate. "I ain't got no trouble talkin' to him."

Jim got up from his saddle and followed Bose over to
where Loving and Goodnight were chatting.

"Pardon, Mr. Lovin'," Bose began, "but Jim here got a
problem he wants to talk to you about."

"Yes, Jim, what is it?" inquired Loving.

"Uh, Mr. Lovin' suh, I, uh—" Jim stuttered.

"Come, boy, say what you have to say," encouraged
Loving.

"Jim's been ridin' drag since we left the ranch," said
Bose, "and he says that the cows that been droppin'
calves all along is causin' him grievous trouble tryin' to
keep them up with the herd."

"Yessuh, that's right," Jim confirmed. "They make me
work all day tryin' to keep them up with the herd."

"That is a problem," said Loving, turning to Goodnight
to include him in the conversation.

"And easily solved," said Goodnight. "Starting with the
first morning after we cross the river, you take your gun
and shoot every newborn calf. Then you do that every
day until this drive is over."

Jim flinched at the command. "Kill them little calfies? I can't do that, Mr. Goodnight."

The hesitation to follow an order irritated Goodnight, and Loving could see the fire stir in his partner's eyes.

"The man say kill them," said Bose, "then you gonna kill them."

"But—"

Then Goodnight broke in. "Look, Jim. I know that it is not an easy thing to do." The softness of his words surprised Loving.

"I just don't like killin' them little calfies, Mr. Goodnight."

"Neither do I," said Goodnight, "but it has to be done."

Jim looked at Loving, who nodded his agreement with his partner. Then he shook his head, saying, "I don't like it, but I guess you is right." He turned and walked away, his head drooping sadly.

"Don't worry, Mr. Goodnight," said Bose. "I'll see that he does what he's told."

"I don't think that will be necessary, Bose," said Goodnight. "Jim appears to be a man who knows his job."

"Yessir, Mr. Goodnight," said Bose, and then he, too, walked away. He quickly caught up with Jim. He tried to offer his friend what solace he could by putting his arm around Fowler's shoulders.

"That Mr. Goodnight is a mean man," said Jim.

"What are you talkin' about, nigger?" demanded Bose in mock anger. "Mr. Goodnight says you is a good man what knows how to do his job."

Jim turned to look at his friend. "That man really say that?"

"That's what the man said," reiterated Bose. "I told him that I would see that you done the job proper, but he say that I don't need to bother, because you is a good man."

"He say I is a good man and not a good nigger?"

"He done called you a man," said Bose. "He never once called you a nigger."

Jim turned around to look back at Goodnight, who was engaged in further discussion with Loving by the fire. "Then, I guess he ain't a mean man after all."

"Come on, Jim," said Bose. "We got to get some rest before we have to stand watch."

The cattle were content that night and all through the next day. The second night and half the second day were the same. Then the time came to head them up and move them out of the cool river valley. With the sun blazing, the cowboys drove the herd into the dry, hot, dusty desert. The afternoon passed without incident, as did the early evening. After dark, when it came time to bed them for the night, there was a noticeable change in the mood of the cattle. They had traveled but a dozen miles, and yet they were already quite thirsty.

"There's gonna be trouble tonight," said Bose when he met up with Jim Fowler on watch. "The steers ain't settlin' down, and the cows what done had calves is more anxious than ever for them."

"Don't look like we gonna get no sleep this night," said Jim. "Uh-oh, there go another one." He rode off to chase a steer back into the herd.

Bose saw a second start for open country in the same direction that they had come from that afternoon. He also rode off to turn back the animal. He and the rest of the cowboys would repeat this action throughout the night, as the cattle refused to settle down.

As soon as the eastern horizon took on a lighter color, Loving gave the order to start the herd moving again. The cowboys welcomed the command. Many of the beeves balked at being driven away from the water that they knew lay behind them, but the wranglers were there to keep them going in the desired direction.

Fifteen miles were covered that day. Loving and Goodnight decided it would be better not to stop until nightfall.

Once again, the longhorns were restless when the stars came out, and the cowhands spent another sleepless night trying to keep them together. Being driven had made the herd thirstier than if they had been left to fend for themselves on the open desert. It was a problem that had to be solved quickly or the drive would be doomed to failure.

"This will never do, Oliver," said Goodnight the next morning. "Those cattle walked enough last night to get them to the Pecos. This camping will not work. I think we should drive them straight through."

"I guess you're right, Charlie," agreed Loving. "I'll pass the word to the boys."

Goodnight stayed with the others that morning instead of going out on his usual scouting forays. It proved to be the hardest day of the drive. Each hour saw steers and cows drop by the wayside to die under a scorching sun. Cowboys fought to stay in their saddles; two sleepless nights and two blistering days had worn them to nearly total exhaustion. Only Goodnight and Bose Ikard seemed tireless among the crew. As the sky lost its colors, they were the only two men not to return to the chuck wagon to refill their canteens and accept a sourdough biscuit from the cook. As the last glow of pink faded on the edge of the world, Bose rode up to the rolling commissary.

"Seen Mr. Goodnight, Bose?" asked Otis Kinney, the camp's cook.

"Not since this afternoon," replied Bose through parched lips.

"Well, he ain't been in yet," said the cook. Otis Kinney was a scrawny, little man with a slight pouch of a belly.

He hid his toothless grin behind a drooping mustache whose ends reached to his chin. He kept his head shaved most of the time, only occasionally allowing the hair to grow out as much as half an inch. "I got an extra biscuit here for him and another canteen. You might take them out to him. I've worked for Mr. Goodnight long enough to know that he neglects his stomach a whole lot. I sometimes wonder if it ain't my cookin' that makes him do that."

Bose smiled although he was weary from the day of trailing. "I don't think that's the reason, Otis. The man is a hard man. He drives himself harder than he does the cattle. Give me that biscuit and water, and I'll make sure he gets them."

Otis handed over the food and drink, and Bose rode off to locate Goodnight. He found him riding drag with Jim Fowler.

"Otis sent me with this here biscuit and canteen, Mr. Goodnight," said Bose as he rode up.

"That Otis is more of a mother hen than a cook," said Goodnight. He halted his work for a moment to chew on the bread and take a large swallow from the canteen. "Of course, he's the best cook I've ever had."

"He sure is a lot better than the one Mr. Lovin' had," said Bose. "That boy couldn't cook a lick. I used to get real hungered when he was messin' with the pots and pans."

"Oh? Who was he, Bose?"

Bose grinned as wide as he could, then said before riding off, "Me."

Goodnight nearly choked on his biscuit as he laughed at the joke. Then he went back to work.

On the third night from the Concho, Goodnight rode the length of the herd, discovering that cattle were strung out for miles. This was bad. It made that much more work for the cowboys as they tried desperately to keep moving. Most of the problem lay in the fact that the men with the drags had no idea where the point was. Goodnight found a solution.

"Fetch me that cowbell," said Goodnight as he rode up to the chuck wagon.

"What in tarnation do you want a cowbell for?" asked Otis Kinney.

"I'm going to use it like ships at sea use bells."

Otis wasn't certain that he had understood his boss correctly, but he retrieved the bell as ordered. He handed it over to the impatient Goodnight.

"Now, when you can't hear this thing ringing," Goodnight continued with his explanation, "then you are too far behind the herd. That means you should move at a faster pace. The same will apply to the drags."

The idea finally got across to Otis. "Why, that's right clever, Mr. Goodnight. Yep, right clever."

"Yes, I know." He rode off for the point, where he found Bose riding in place of Billy Wilson. "Where's Billy?"

"He done fell asleep, Mr. Goodnight," said Bose. "So I took his spot till he got some rest."

Goodnight was studious for a moment. He had known Wilson since before the war. Folks called him "One-armed" Billy, because his left arm was deformed from birth; it didn't develop completely. Despite the inconvenience of having one arm that could do only a third as much as the other, Billy had always carried his own loads. Goodnight knew him as a man who could be expected to do his job better than most. Now that he needed him more than ever, the rancher wondered if that trust had been placed properly.

"You want me to get him for you, Mr. Goodnight?"

Goodnight shook his head. "No, let him have his rest. God knows that all of you need it."

"Not me, Mr. Goodnight," Bose smiled.

Goodnight could see that Bose was not boasting idly. "I have a job for you, Bose." Without further hesitation, he handed the bell to Bose. "Here, tie this around your horse's neck. Then you stay here on point till we reach the Pecos."

"But what about Billy?"

"I'll have him elsewhere for the time being."

"Yessir, Mr. Goodnight, if that's what you want."

That was exactly what Goodnight wanted, and Bose rode the point for the remaining thirty miles to the river, a full night and day away.

It was around two the next morning when trouble came in bunches to the cowboys. The herd was approaching Castle Canyon when a cool breeze blew up in their faces. The leaders took one smell of that wind and thought that water was close by. A few let out bawls, and the others seemed to understand exactly what they meant. Before Bose and Jake, the other point rider, realized what was about to happen, they were off at a trot to quench their thirst.

Bose kicked his horse into action, and the cowbell began to clang out a warning to all those behind that something was amiss at the point. Jake had been dozing, but the clatter of the bell bolted him into a frenzied response. The two wranglers rode in and out of the herd trying to head off the leaders, but neither could do much to sway them from stampeding. They slowed a few, but only momentarily. Help was needed if a full-fledged break was to be avoided.

It wasn't long in coming as Goodnight and Billy Wilson joined the melee. Wilson charged his horse into the side of one small steer, causing it to stumble. Other cattle

behind it tried to sidestep the fallen animal, slowing their
progress as they did. Goodnight attempted to do the
same, but the longhorn he singled out to bump proved
readier for the jolt. It bawled as it bounced off the cowman's coal-black mare, then, maddened by thirst, it
charged. Horse and rider toppled to the ground, with
Goodnight being thrown clear of his mount. He started to
reach for the reins as the mare struggled to regain her
footing, but then he saw the steer coming after him with
horns lowered.

Bose had been knocking leaders just the same as the
others, but he had caught Goodnight's fall out of the
corner of his eye. He turned his mount to ride to the
fallen man's aid. The steer made its charge. Bose kicked
his horse as hard as he could, and the animal leaped
ahead on a course that would put it between Goodnight
and the longhorn. Just at the right instant, Bose jumped
from his saddle, landing full force on the beast's head and
right between its horns. The animal was unprepared for
the extra weight on its neck. Its nose dug into the sand,
and its body flipped forward and over Bose, crashing to
the ground short of Goodnight. Bose's momentum rolled
him against the prostrate steer. Although the neck was
broken, the hooves thrashed wildly at anything and at
nothing. It appeared to Goodnight that Bose had been
kicked, and the cowman rushed to the side of the black
cowboy who had just saved his life.

"Bose, are you all right?" Goodnight was frantic as he
knelt beside the wrangler.

Bose rolled over, a smile on his lips. "Did you see
which way my hoss went?" He sprang to his feet. "I'd
hate to lose that hoss."

Goodnight shook his head, wondering how this Negro
lad could come so close to death and not be shaken by it.

He wouldn't question Bose about it, feeling that it would only serve to lessen the deed done.

"I got him," said Jake as he rode up with the animal in tow. "Dumb nigger. You best be more careful how y'all treat Mr. Lovin's stock."

"Sure thing, Jake," said Bose as he slapped the dust from his clothes. Taking the reins from his friend, he climbed back into the saddle. He looked about to see that the herd had been brought to a standstill. "Looks like you got the job done, Jake."

"No thanks to you. Some of us was workin' while y'all were playin' tug-o'-war with that steer. Now get back over there where you belong, and keep that bell quiet. I'm tryin' to get me some sleep."

Goodnight listened and learned. Oliver Loving had good men working for him, no matter what their color was.

When the sun rose that morning, Goodnight took a fresh mount from the remuda and rode from man to man, gathering their canteens. When he passed the chuck wagon, he had a few short words for Otis Kinney.

"Catch up with Bose at the point and see that he gets a biscuit or two. Then head straight for the Pecos. I'm going there now for more water. When you get to the river, stay on this side and make camp high above the valley. I want these men to have a hot meal come sundown."

Otis understood his instructions completely, nodding so before Goodnight departed. He stepped up the pace of the mules pulling his rig. The mules, unlike cattle and horses, were able to withstand the rigors of the desert crossing enough so that they could take a faster speed. It took them less than an hour to haul the chuck wagon to the point of the herd, where Kinney found Bose, the cowbell still clanging its signal to those behind him.

"Here," said Kinney as he offered Bose a biscuit. "Mr.

Goodnight said to make sure you got fed this morning."

"That was kind of him," said Bose. He accepted the food and bit off a corner. He chewed slowly as his mouth was having trouble delivering any saliva. "This is the driest biscuit you ever made, Otis."

"Well, there ain't nobody makin' you eat it." Otis whipped the mules with one flick of the lash. "See you at the river tonight."

It was the third day that the cattle had been without water. The beasts had become crazed with thirst. It was late that morning when Goodnight returned with the filled canteens. He passed among the men, handing each one the welcome refreshment, until he reached Loving working with the drags.

"The river is only ten miles ahead," said Goodnight. "The leaders will be smelling it before too long. I think I'll take the horses and some of the men and let the herd have its way. You bring up the drags as best as you can."

Loving's throat was parched to the point that it hurt to talk. A long swallow from the canteen eased the pain as well as the dryness.

"We'll carry on, Charlie," said Loving. "Good luck, and I'll see you at the river."

By the time Goodnight returned to the point, the leaders had already quickened their pace, having caught a whiff of the water ahead. Bose and Jake were trying to slow them as Goodnight intervened.

"Let them run," he said to Bose. "You stand aside and let as many pass as want to. When you see Mr. Loving bringing up the drags, come ahead with him. Hold most of the men behind, because there could be danger if the herd gets too wild."

Bose nodded, then pulled his horse to one side of the herd. He watched as Goodnight, Wilson, Tatum, and Willborn drove the horses to the front at a gallop. Then the leaders broke into a run. Gradually, all the stronger cattle followed them. Water was still a long way off, but they would die to get to it.

It was an hour later that Loving came up with the drags. Bose estimated that there were five hundred head left. They stumbled along at an unsteady gait, some falling and never rising again. Covered with dust, Loving waved a tired hand as a signal for everyone to move with the stragglers. They reached the river an hour before the sun went mercifully down.

That particular part of the Pecos was guarded on each side by steep, ditch-like banks. From seeing a few bloated bodies lying along the water's edge, Bose could imagine how the cattle had rushed over the banks to get to the river. Some had probably been killed in the fall, while others drowned. The longhorns that had survived were spread out across the whole breadth of the Pecos and for half a mile up- and downstream. The drags only added to the confusion.

"Keep them away from the alkali ponds," warned Goodnight as he rode up to Loving and Ikard. "They seem to be behind every bush. We've lost enough without letting them kill themselves on that poison."

Bose and the remaining cowboys drove the stragglers down to the water, allowing their horses to drink too. All had thought they would be given a much needed rest as soon as they reached the river, but it wasn't yet to be. Instead they were told to drive the cattle away from certain parts of the riverbed because of dangerous quicksand. They worked well into the night chasing steers and cows back up the steep banks to the grassy flatlands that paralleled the river. It was almost midnight before the cowboys had the last of the herd safely out of the water.

Otis Kinney had followed his employer's orders to the ultimate. He had prepared a fine cowboy repast of beef, baked beans, and sourdough biscuits with honey. As hungry as they were, the wranglers were too worn out to eat. Some managed a few bites before drifting off to sleep, their eating utensils still in their hands and on their laps. The others had the midnight watch. They fell asleep in their saddles as their horses kept the lonely vigil for them.

Under any other conditions, Kinney would have become angry at the men for letting his food take second place to sleep. But he was too exhausted himself to make any bones about it. After taking the meat and beans from the fire, he retired to his bedroll beneath the wagon.

Only Bose Ikard and Charlie Goodnight remained awake that night. Each man slowly circled the herd, disturbing neither the cattle nor the other cowboys. The worst of the drive was over, and both were glad of it.

FIVE

Goodnight and Loving agreed that the men, as well as the herd and the remuda of horses, had earned a solid respite from the harshness of the trail. Of course, there was still work to be done, but it wasn't the same, punishing brand of labor the desert crossing had demanded. The cattle that had managed to mire themselves in the quicksand bottoms of the Pecos had to be pulled free, or at least the attempt had to be made. Strays had to be recruited, but, more important for the days ahead, the beasts had to be tamed all over again.

After three days of seemingly easy tasks, the trail herd was on the move again as the cowboys headed them north along the river toward Fort Sumner and the Bosque Redondo.

They forded the Pecos at Horsehead Crossing, so named because legend said that a raiding party of Comanches coming back from Mexico had driven their horses so hard that many of them died there from drinking water from the alkali-infested pools that dot the Pecos Valley. It was further told that the Comanches butchered the animals, leaving their skulls as a constant reminder to all travelers that death lurks at the bottoms of those deceivingly limpid ponds.

Driving up the west bank of the river until they reached Pope's Crossing, the cowboys returned the herd to the east side, because Goodnight thought it wise to place the Pecos between them and the Guadalupe Mountains. It was a known fact that the Mescalero Apaches rendezvoused there each summer, and Goodnight could see no reason to make the stock and men a part of that event.

At Fort Sumner, the cowmen found a ready market for their beeves. The military post had been built a few years earlier for the sole purpose of keeping the Navajos and Mimbres Apaches on their God-forsaken reservation, the Bosque Redondo. Since the reservation lands were so poor, the Army was forced to feed the Indians. Texas cattle were rapidly becoming the main course on the Indians' menu, whether they came from honest ranchers like Goodnight and Loving or from the Comancheros, the brigands of the Plains, who had stolen them or who had traded for them with the Comanches and Kiowas.

The Army bought only steers, leaving Goodnight and Loving with a smaller herd of cows, bulls, and calves. This presented the partners with a slight problem, which they discussed by the light of their campfire late one evening in early July.

"It was our original intention to take the herd to Colorado," reminded Loving as he poured himself a cup of steaming coffee from the blackened pot next to the fire. "We can still do that. I feel certain that we will find as good a market there as here."

"Yes, I agree," said Goodnight, "but it would be a waste to have eighteen men drive such a small herd up there."

"Then, what do you suggest?"

Goodnight was pensive before answering. Absentmindedly, he tugged at one end of his mustache with a gloved hand. His lower lip twitched in thought. Loving waited patiently.

"I believe it would be a wise thing to divide the men between us," offered Goodnight. "I could take, say, three with me and return to Texas for another herd. We can cut straight through the Comanche country riding by night and holing up by day. That would make the trip shorter. It shouldn't take but a few days to round up another crew and gather a herd. I can have them back here before autumn.

"In the meantime, you take the rest of the outfit and the remainder of the stock up to Colorado. Sell the herd to the highest bidder, then come back here. You can give the men the option of staying on or going about their own business."

Loving approved the plan, and the next day the two men bade each other farewell, each wishing the other good fortune and a safe passage.

Bose Ikard remained with Loving, riding point as they headed north for the mining districts around Denver. The miners would pay almost any price for a beefsteak. Loving was quite aware of that fact as he drove hard bargains with every buyer that approached him. When John Wesley Iliff came forward with an offer to buy the entire lot, Loving gladly accepted the deal, which included delivery at Iliff's budding ranch north of Denver on the South Platte River.

Iliff invited Loving and his crew to remain as guests on his ranch for a few days, but Loving was hesitant to accept his hospitality because of the appointed rendezvous with Goodnight at Fort Sumner. The cowboys got wind of the invitation and Loving's polite refusal. The thought of making another hard ride back to New Mexico without the chance to sample a few of the delights of Denver caused a mild revolt among the hired men.

"Mr. Lovin', we been talkin'," said Jake, acting as spokesman for the wranglers, "and we was thinkin' that we'd like to spend some of our money down in Denver before goin' back to Sumner. There ain't a whole lot of us that's ever been to a place like that before. We'd kinda like to see what it's all about."

Loving didn't hold with cowboys drinking and gambling and carousing the streets of towns, but he knew he would have to grant them their request if he was to keep them together. He had to go to Denver anyway to deposit the money from the cattle sales in a bank. He had only planned to take Bose and Jake with him, but seeing the mood the rest of them were in, he relented.

The outfit made a procession as Loving led them through the streets of Denver, somewhat to the amusement of its citizenry. Texas cowpunchers were an unfamiliar sight, one that provoked ladies to whisper and giggle and gentlemen to nudge each other in the ribs and guffaw. The cowboys ignored the curious stares and raucous laughter, as their attention was drawn to the surrounding buildings.

Denver was a very young city, still experiencing the labor pains of premature birth. Fine homes and buildings to house all the new people and businesses were springing up on every street as carpenters cut their lumber and drove their nails and as masons mixed their mortar and laid their bricks. Since the railroad was slow in reaching the Colorado capital, teamsters raced everywhere, either delivering some commodity that was always in short supply or rushing back to the railhead at Julesburg for another load.

The Texans, Bose in particular, were awed by every little thing. Never before had they seen so many people congregated at one time in one place. The speed with which everyone dashed about astounded them. They wondered what pressing engagements caused these folk to hurry so.

And the noise! After the soundless breezes of the grasslands, which were broken only by the occasional bawling of the cattle, the pounding of hammers, the rattling of wagons, and the shouts of men hard at work were deafening to their ears, bringing a muteness to their throats.

Surely they would have turned tail and run had not one thought maintained their sanity for them. Somewhere in that city there was a saloon with warm beer, rotgut whiskey, and friendly ladies of the evening, waiting just for them.

Loving turned his horse onto one of Denver's few cobblestone streets. Straight ahead he saw a sign hanging out over the sidewalk designating the Brown Hotel. Directly across the street was the Bank of Denver. The hostelry appeared to be a respectable establishment, one quite suited to his tastes. He turned his horse aside, planning to tie it to the rail in front of the building.

"Hold on a minute, Mr. Lovin'," said Jake, his voice tinged with panic. "This place looks to be a might too fancy for the likes of us. Maybe we better find us a hotel that's a little more fittin'."

Loving scanned the faces of the cowboys. "You might be right about that, Jake. You boys don't have to stay here if you don't want to. You each have your own money, so you can go where you please. Just remember one thing. Tomorrow morning at sunup, I will be riding out of this town for New Mexico. Those of you who want to remain in my employ will meet me here in front of this hotel at that time. If you're late, don't bother trying to catch up. Is that perfectly clear?"

Jake spoke up as if he were still speaking for every man in the crew. "Yessir, Mr. Lovin'. Sunup tomorrow. We'll be here, won't we, boys?"

There was a murmur of consent from the wranglers and a few nods. Loving was satisfied as he waved them on their way, knowing full well that they were headed for a

less reputable part of town. He was surprised to see Bose
staying behind with him.

"Why aren't you going with the others, Bose?"

"I figure you need someone to help watch over things,
Mr. Lovin'." Bose's eyes shifted to the saddlebags on the
croup of Loving's horse. "Maybe I can see that every single thing comes out the way it should."

"Yes, I quite agree, Bose." Loving patted the bags that
held all the money he had in the world. "Would you
mind sharing a room with me?" He was alit before Bose
could answer. "There's nothing to be concerned with
here. You are with me, and that's all that matters."

"If you say so, Mr. Lovin'."

Bose dismounted and followed Loving inside the hotel.
The lobby was occupied by a half dozen men, each
dressed stylishly in the latest of men's suits. Loving appeared to be out of place in his linen duster, and Bose
was even more so in his denim pants and cotton shirt.
Their Texas boots rapped out a tattoo on the hardwood
floor, drawing the attention of every person in the room,
especially the desk clerk, who waited nervously for the
Texans to step to the counter to register. Bose could feel
the stares boring through him as he watched Loving
reach for the pen to sign his name in the registry.

"I'll have a room for one night," said Loving. "One
with a bath." He inked his name in the book. "And two
beds, if you have them."

"We're all filled," quaked the clerk.

The cattleman replaced the pen in its holder and glowered at the shaking little man behind the counter. "All
filled, you say? I find that to be strange, sir, since I see so
many keys hanging from those hooks behind you."

"Those are extra keys," said the clerk hurriedly. Beads
of perspiration blossomed from his eyebrows to his reced-

ing hairline. His fingers tapped a spasmodic rhythm on the desk.

"I find that highly unlikely," countered Loving.

"Sir, I don't think you understand," rejoined the clerk.

"I understand perfectly. You are refusing me a room because my friend here is colored. Is that not so?"

"Well, no, sir, it's, uh—"

"Pardon me, sir," came another man's voice from behind the Texans.

They turned to see a tall man with dark hair and a matching mustache approaching them. Superbly dressed in a dark blue suit but not carrying or wearing a hat, the man stepped with an air of importance, which suggested that he might be the hotel's owner or manager.

"Yes?" said Loving as simply as he could.

"Might I inquire about where you hail from, sir?" asked the gentleman.

"I am from Texas, sir," replied Loving with pride.

"So I might have gathered. It would seem that you Texans are not yet fully aware that slavery has been done away with throughout this great land of ours."

Loving was incensed by the accusation, but before he could react, Bose stepped to the fore.

"I ain't no slave, mister," Bose growled through clenched teeth. "I work for Mr. Lovin' by my own choice, and I get paid real good for it too." Bose allowed his right hand to rest on the grip of the Colt at his side while he reached into a vest pocket with the other to pull out a few coins. "See here at this money that's all mine? I earned it ridin' for Mr. Lovin'." He returned the money to its place and patted his gun. "Now, if you don't mind, Mr. Lovin' wants a room."

"One moment, Bose," said Loving. He stepped closer to the rude gentleman. "Might I inquire about who you are, sir?"

The man nervously twisted the knot of his tie and cleared his throat before answering. "I am Edward Brown. I manage this establishment for my brother."

"And a fine establishment it is, Mr. Brown. One that I will recommend to all my friends, but only if the manners of the hired help improve. Now, how about that room?"

Brown looked past Loving to the desk clerk. "See that these gentlemen are well taken care of, Gibbons. Give them the best room available."

"Yes, sir, Mr. Brown," said Gibbons as he spun around to find the right key for their room. Then he just as quickly did another about-face. "Here you are, Mr. Loving. Second floor and in the middle of the hall. The room faces the street."

Loving snapped up the key before turning back to Brown. "Things are improving already, Mr. Brown. Yes, a very fine establishment. Shall we go, Bose?"

"I best see about the hosses, Mr. Lovin'," said Bose as he made a move for the door.

"Never mind that, Bose. Mr. Brown will see to them, won't you, sir? The two bays tied up side by side out front. I'd like them quartered at the nearest livery, if you don't mind."

Brown was irritated, but he held his temper. "As you wish, Mr. Loving."

"Fine," said Loving, more pleased with himself for putting the manager in his proper place than he was with the man's cooperation. "Yes, indeed, a fine establishment."

Loving stepped haughtily past Brown and led Bose up to their room. An hour later, they walked across the street to deposit the money from the sales of the cattle. When that chore was finished, they went out on the sidewalk, unsure of what to do next.

"Well, Bose, I think I would like to see more of this city before it gets dark," said Loving as he surveyed first

in one direction, then in the other. "You can either stay
with me or you can go find the rest of the boys and join
them in whatever merriment they might be up to by
now."

"I'll walk with you a piece, Mr. Lovin'. I ain't so sure I
can find my way around this here town."

Loving laughed. "I see what you mean, Bose. It is a
rather large city, isn't it?"

"It sure is, Mr. Lovin'. It sure is."

The afternoon passed quickly as they went from store
to store, looking at everything from ladies' fashions to the
newest rifles and handguns from back East. Denver was a
curious sight to Bose, but Bose was an equally curious
sight to Denver. Although most of the citizens had seen
blacks at one time or another, few of them had ever met
one close up. Bose was ignorant of that fact, but Loving
was incensed by the stares and the cold conversations
they received from shop clerks and people on the streets.
He figured, however, that since Bose seemed to be un-
touched by their offensive behavior that he, too, would ig-
nore them.

After purchasing a new Winchester .44 carbine from
M. L. Rood's gun shop, Loving heard the sounds of gaiety
coming from the next street over. With the sun resting on
the peaks of the Rockies, he decided it was a fitting time
of the day for a drink or two. He led Bose to the Belmont
Saloon.

"Mr. Lovin'!" came a familiar voice when Loving entered through the swinging doors. It was Jake, leaning
against the bar, a shot glass in his hand. "Come on over
here and let me buy y'all a drink." Then he spotted Bose
behind his boss. "You, too, Bose. I 'specially want to buy
you a drink. Bartender, set 'em up for my boss and the
best damned cowboy in Texas."

They joined Jake at the bar, and Loving ordered two

beers for Bose and himself. It was quite evident by the odor of his breath and the glaze in his eyes that Jake had already spent a lot of his cash. Loving wondered if he had done the right thing by turning his crew loose on the saloons of Denver.

"Drink up, Bose," said Jake as the bartender set two mugs of beer in front of the new arrivals.

Bose watched Loving blow the head from his beer, then he tried it. The result was the same, but Bose lacked the finesse of Loving as the foam sprayed instead of spread over the rim of the mug. Loving poured half the beer down his throat before coming up for air. Bose hardly got past the first taste, as the beer was warm and bitter, causing a frown to contort his face.

"This stuff is awful bad," said Bose after wiping his mouth on his sleeve.

"That's only the first taste," said Jake. "Take another one. It won't be so bad this time."

"No, I think this here stuff is bad for me," said Bose. "It don't taste so good, and if it's gonna do to me what it done to you already, then I don't want no part of it."

"That's a very sensible decision, Bose," said Loving. "There are many other ways to enjoy oneself besides drinking your fill of beer or hard liquor."

"Y'all can say that again," said Jake.

Bose was surprised to hear those words coming from Tatum. He turned to look at him but saw that Jake was focusing his eyes on something else, the reason for his statement. Coming down the stairs were two saloon girls. One was blond and had the whitest skin that he had ever seen. Her blue eyes fairly sparkled above her rouged cheeks. Her low-cut dress helped to accentuate her figure, as the stays in it pushed everything out beyond their real proportions. Pink ruffles at the hem of the red and black gown hid her knees but exposed black-stockinged calves and ankles. She was really a wonder to behold, thought Bose, but the other girl made an even greater impression on him. Her black hair and chestnut eyes glistened like silk. The dress she wore was cut the same way as the blonde's, but that still didn't interest Bose as much as the milk-chocolate texture of her skin. She was the first black girl he had seen since his days in Shantytown.

"Now, there is a beautiful sight if I ever did see one," said Jake. "Will y'all just look at that? Ain't they somethin'?"

No one was arguing with him, but no one was agreeing with him either. He turned to see Bose enraptured by the view. He nudged Loving, then nodded toward Bose, once he had his employer's attention.

"Like what you see, Bose?" asked Loving, an elfish lilt in his voice. He wondered if Bose could withstand the wily charms of a lady of the evening as well as he had resisted the draft of beer.

"What's that you said, Mr. Lovin'?" Bose was mildly embarrassed. "You talkin' about them ladies?"

"That's right. Do you like them?"

Bose couldn't stop a sheepish grin from breaking out all over his face. "Yessir, they sure is purty."

"Would you like one to come over and talk to you?" asked Loving.

"I sure would," said Jake, "but I ain't gonna wait." He staggered over to the staircase to meet the girls at its foot.

"Why don't you go with him, Bose?" suggested Loving.

Bose shied his face away from his boss. "Aw, that girl don't want to talk to no cowboy like me."

"Sure she does," insisted Loving. "Listen, I'll go ask her for you. You go sit yourself at that table over there, and I'll send her over to you."

Bose looked up at the girls again. "You sure she gonna come over and talk to me?"

"Trust me, Bose, she will. Now, go over there and have a seat."

Even as he walked to the table, Bose kept his eyes on the two girls, especially the black one. She was the most beautiful woman that he had ever seen, and he wanted to see more of her but at closer inspection.

He watched Loving step up alongside Jake at the bottom of the stairs. A few words were exchanged which he couldn't hear, but he did see Loving hand the black girl a gold coin. She took the money and put it into a pocket inside the front of her dress. Loving moved aside, and she took the last step to the barroom floor and crossed the room to Bose's table.

"That man over there said you need someone to be nice to you," she said as she slipped her arms around Bose's neck. "Is that what you need, cowboy?"

Bose could feel the sweat beads popping out all over him. The girl removed his hat and placed it on the table. Her perfume permeated his nostrils, and the fragrance set a blaze in him that he didn't know existed until that very moment.

"What's your name, cowboy?"

"Bose!" He surprised himself by spitting out his own name. "Uh, Bose Ikard," he said in a calmer tone.

"What kind of name is that?" she teased.

"What's your name, girl?" demanded Bose.

"Around here, they call me Ebony, but my real name is Hannah." She leaned back, wondering why she had told him that.

"I like Hannah," said Bose. "Used to have a milk cow named Hannah. She sure was a good cow."

"Are you callin' me a cow?" Hannah snarled. "'Cause if you are, I'll give that man his money back."

Bose ignored her complaint. "Knew a white lady named Hannah, too. She wasn't near as purty as you are."

"Now, that's more like what a girl likes to hear," said Hannah, doing an instant turnaround. "Would you like to buy me a drink?"

"Nope. Drinkin' ain't for ladies. It ain't for me neither."

"Well, then, what would you like to do?"

"I don't know," said Bose.

"Well, I do," said Hannah as she took his hand. "Come on with me, and I'll show you."

"Where we goin'?" demanded Bose as he was jerked to his feet.

"We're goin' to my room," explained Hannah as she tugged at his arm.

"What for?"

"You'll see," she said as she pulled him toward the stairs.

Bose reached back in time to grab his hat, then let Hannah have her way. He looked about the barroom for Jake and Loving. Jake had disappeared with the blonde, but Loving was back at the bar. He waved and smiled, and Bose figured that whatever Hannah had in mind was all right with his employer; therefore, it was all right with him.

"This where you live?" asked Bose, once they were in Hannah's room upstairs. He was surprised by the decor. The bed had a pink satin cover with matching pillows. Ornate kerosene lamps sat on two nightstands, which stood on each side of the headboard. A picture of a nude lady was hanging on the wall above the bed. There seemed to be mirrors at every turn. Decanters of whiskey were mixed with bottles of perfume and cosmetics on the dresser. There were two other doors besides the one that led from the hall. One was a closet, and the other had glass in it and drapes over it, leading to the balcony on the front of the saloon.

"Yes, I live here," said Hannah. "Do you like it?"

"This sure is some nice room," said Bose as he turned away from her and walked over to the dresser. "You drink this here whiskey?" He picked up a bottle and turned to show it to Hannah. The container fell from his grasp but didn't break when it hit the carpeted floor. Bose, however, nearly went to pieces when he saw that Hannah had her dress half off. "What are you doin', girl?"

"What's it look like I'm doin'?"

Bose was dumfounded as he watched her, his eyes bulging and his mouth hanging open. A hard swallow brought him back to reality. "Put this here dress back on!" He waited a moment before repeating the order. "Put it on."

Hannah was surprised by his attitude. Although she was a year younger than Bose, she had had enough experience in the world to realize that he was totally innocent.

"Ain't you never been with a gal before?" she asked. There was understanding in her eyes and a softening in her heart. "This is your first time, ain't it?"

"Nope," said Bose as a fire ignited in his charcoal face. "This ain't the first time. I ain't done this before, and I ain't gonna start now. My mammy brung me up on the good book, and I know this is sinnin'."

Hannah wasn't interested in any Sunday school lectures, but she was struck by something that Bose said. "You knew your mammy? For real, you knew her?"

"Course I knowed my mammy. What kinda fool question is that?"

"I didn't know mine," confessed Hannah, a shadow dulling her face. Then she remembered what her profession was. "Now, look here, cowboy. The man downstairs already paid me, and now I got to give."

"Not to me, you don't. That ain't why I come up here."

"Then, why did you come up here?"

"You're the purtiest gal I ever did see, Hannah. I just want to talk with you."

"Just talk?"

Bose nodded.

"Ain't no one ever just want to talk to me before. What did you say your name was?"

"Bose Ikard."

"Well, Bose Ikard, let's talk," she said as she sat down on the bed. Bose looked around for a place to sit. "You can sit here with me, Bose. I promise not to do anything but talk." Bose hesitated. "I promise, Bose." He started to seat himself, but the dress caught his eye again. "Oh, all right, I'll put it back on." Hannah climbed back into the gown, and Bose sat down next to her.

"That's better," said Bose. "Now I feel more at ease."

An hour passed, in which they told each other almost everything general there was to tell about their individual lives. They would have continued, but a knock at the door reminded Hannah that other customers would be waiting.

"How come you do this?" asked Bose.

"I ain't got no other way to make money," Hannah sighed.

"You don't like it. I can tell that."

"No, I guess I don't." Bose started to say something, but she cut him short. "You're a good-lookin' man, Bose, and I like you because you're nice to me too. But there ain't nothin' you can do about this, so why don't you just go and leave me be what I am."

Bose didn't like that idea, but he couldn't see any reason to argue about it at that time. "Can I see you again?"

Hannah shrugged. "You can see me all you want as long as you pay the money." She nudged him toward the door.

"I didn't mean that way," said Bose. "I meant I want to see you away from this place."

"Bose, I don't ever get away from this place. If you want to see me, you'll have to see me here."

"Then, if I has to pay the money," he said quickly, "then I will."

"Fine," said Hannah. "Now good-bye, Bose."

He stepped into the hall, not realizing that a long winter would pass before he would get a chance to spend his money for Hannah.

SIX

By mid-October, the Goodnight-Loving outfit was settled in winter quarters on the Bosque. To that point in time, the partners had experienced little difficulty in carrying out any of their plans. Their rendezvous at Fort Sumner in September had actually come off better than they had hoped. Goodnight's second drive from Texas was easier than the first, mostly because the herd consisted entirely of steers instead of being mixed with cows and bulls.

Upon hearing of Goodnight's initial success, other Texas cattlemen tried their luck with the same trail. Not all achieved their goal, some because they were unwise in the ways of the cattle drive and others because the Comanches had also heard of the new route.

Although competition for Army contracts had increased, Goodnight and Loving realized bigger profits with the second herd. The money didn't come as fast, but it was steady, as the partners made monthly deliveries of one hundred head each to the military post. In addition, Loving had secured a deal to deliver another hundred beeves each month to two butchers in Santa Fe. Filling the two orders kept the outfit from complete boredom throughout the winter.

Goodnight had chosen a spot on the east bank of the Pecos to build some crude huts of sod and mud for their ranch on the Bosque range. The men didn't care for the work, but the first blast of chilling wind down from the Rockies made them appreciate the little soddies. The only times they left the shelters and their constant card games were when the two hundred head had to be rounded up for the deliveries to Sumner and Santa Fe. Neither Loving nor Goodnight approved of gambling, so the cowboys played a lot of whist and rummy that season.

One problem did arise that caused some excitement for the outfit. They awoke one morning to discover half the horses and mules were missing from the remuda. Until that day, the animals had been permitted to roam the hills near the ranch, making their theft easy. When it was discovered that one of the missing mounts was Goodnight's favorite saddle horse, Bose was chosen to tell him about the loss. It was generally felt that he could talk to the bosses better than any other man.

"Good morning, Bose," said Goodnight, not suspecting any trouble. "What brings you up here so early in the day?"

"Mr. Goodnight," Bose began as he interrupted the partners in the middle of their breakfast inside their quarters, "we got to put a guard on the remuda at night. It might be best that we put the hosses and mules in a corral, too."

"Why is that, Bose?" asked Goodnight, still not sure of what Bose was getting at.

"Well, sir, it looks like the Injuns done made off with half the stock last night, includin' your best hoss."

"What's this?" demanded Goodnight. He dropped his fork on the table in front of him. Loving also ceased to consume the repast of bacon and biscuits.

"Are you certain of this, Bose?" asked Loving.

"Yessir. We done checked to see which hosses was missin'. Them Injuns musta took half the herd."

The partners were out of their chairs and into their coats before Bose could offer further information. They burst through the doorway and raced down the hill to where the men were gathered outside their huts. Bose ran behind but kept pace with them.

"All right," said Goodnight calmly after briefly surveying the scene. "Anyone see any sign?" No one spoke up. "Then, it must have been Indians. Everyone mount up on whatever horses we have left. We're going after those dirty savages. I want my horse back."

Without waiting to be told twice, the cowboys were in the saddle and following Goodnight's lead. They rode to the top of the bluff to scan the countryside around the ranch. Goodnight had a keen eye, but he knew that Bose had even better eyesight.

"You see anything, Bose?" he asked.

"Nope. Looks to me like they covered their tracks real good."

"So it would seem, Bose, but thieves always leave some sort of sign. We'll spread out from here and take a good look." Goodnight made a sweeping motion with his arm. "I want every inch of this ground covered. If anyone finds any sign, holler over to the man next to you and pass the word. Do not fire your guns. I want those Indians to think they got away with it clean. Now move."

The cowboys fanned out as Goodnight directed them. The half circle that they created grew steadily larger as the morning wore on. Each man had a wedge of prairie to search, and he worked that wedge back and forth in ever-lengthening and zigzagging paths. It was near noon when Goodnight himself found the sign he was looking for. He shouted for the others to join him, and fifteen minutes elapsed before all the wranglers and Goodnight were following the trail left by the Indians.

"It heads almost due north," said Goodnight in passing. "Makes me think it had to be Navajos. At first, I thought it was Comanches, but I didn't think they would come this far just to steal a few horses and mules. They would have taken the cattle, too. None of them seem to be missing."

"Hold on, Mr. Goodnight," said Bose. "I see some riders up ahead. Don't look like Injuns to me. 'Pears to be bluecoats."

Goodnight studied the terrain ahead of them. "I believe you are correct, Bose. They seem to be riding in formation, and that does suggest that they are soldiers. I think we should have a talk with these Yankees."

Goodnight spurred his horse into a trot, and his men followed suit. Minutes later, they were face to face with a detachment of cavalry from Fort Sumner.

"Good afternoon, sir," said the young lieutenant at the head of the patrol. "You are Mr. Goodnight, are you not, sir?"

"I am the same," Goodnight replied.

The officer saluted. "Lieutenant Robert Collins at your service, sir. Might I inquire as to why you and your men are on the reservation?"

"Indeed you may, sir," said Goodnight. "We're on the trail of the Indians who raided my ranch last night and made off with some horses and mules."

"Have you reported this incident to the post commander, Mr. Goodnight?"

"I have not yet had the opportunity to make the complaint."

"Then, consider it made, sir," said Collins. "It would seem that we are both after the same quarry. A small band of young Navajo braves were discovered missing this morning. Eight in all. It would seem that they are the same that raided your ranch in the night."

"Then, we shouldn't have any trouble finding them," said Goodnight. "My men are at your disposal, Mr. Collins."

"Pardon me, sir," said Collins, not pleased with the

turn of events, "but I will have to ask you and your men to turn back. This is the reservation, and civilians are not permitted—"

"No further explanation is needed, Lieutenant," interrupted Goodnight. "Now that I know the Army is on the chase I will gladly retire." Goodnight started to turn away, but then he had a second thought. "Would you permit me to ride with you? They took my favorite horse, and I would like to see it returned."

"Can you identify all your stock, Mr. Goodnight?"

"By their brands, I can."

"They ain't all got your brand, Mr. Goodnight," interjected Bose. "Some of them is from that bunch you just bought last week, and we ain't got around to brandin' them yet."

Goodnight was unperturbed. "Would you recognize those horses, Bose?"

"Yessir, I know them all."

"Then, Lieutenant, would it be all right if both of us rode with you?" asked Goodnight.

"Certainly, sir," said Collins without hesitation.

Goodnight sent the others back to the ranch with specific orders to begin constructing a corral immediately and to get the horses rounded up and moved closer to the ranch until the fence was finished. Then he joined Collins at the head of the column as they rode after the Indians. Bose rode ahead as he scouted the slight trail left by the raiding Navajos.

They followed the sign until late in the day. Bose continued to lead the way. When he came to the edge of a wide ravine, he halted his horse and dismounted. He had found what they were searching for. He was kneeling beside his mount when Goodnight and the cavalry rode up. The cowman scanned the gully.

"Dirty buggers!" he swore. He jumped from his horse

as Collins stopped the troopers behind him. "They will pay for this."

"Yours are not the first," said Collins, still in the saddle. "Nearly every ranch in this area has been raided in the same fashion and with the same results."

"Well, they won't be raiding my ranch again," vowed Goodnight. He knelt down on one knee beside Bose. A gloved hand wiped his face. "Never again! If I so much as see a Navajo on my ranch, I will shoot him myself. They'll pay for this."

Bose and Goodnight mounted their horses and rode down into the ravine for a closer inspection. Collins nudged his mount to follow them. Quietly, the three men walked their steeds through the area where the Navajos had paused to butcher the stolen animals. Bose counted the hides and heads, matching them with the few entrails that lay near each one.

"Looks like they gonna eat all but the snort," said Bose. "Don't see why they want to eat hosses and mules. There was plenty of cattle they coulda took. Why do they want to steal hosses and eat them?"

"The Navajos prefer horsemeat to beef," explained Collins. "It does appear to be a strange diet, but what else would one expect from savages?"

Goodnight rode around the remains of the stock. "Looks like more than eight men rode off from here, Mr. Collins. I count at least a dozen ponies."

"It would seem that they had assistance," said Collins. "There is little we can do about this now."

"Yes, it would seem so," agreed Goodnight. Most cattlemen would have demanded remuneration from the Army for such a loss, but most weren't doing so much business with the military. "But, mark my words, Mr. Collins. I will not let them take another horse from me. They will have to kill me first."

"You don't plan to institute any legal action, do you, Mr. Goodnight?"

"No, I do not, Lieutenant. I will honor the boundaries of the reservation, but if the Navajos come near my ranch, I will shoot them or have them shot. You may pass that warning to your commanding officer, and he may pass it to the Navajos."

"I shall do that, sir. We shall be returning to the post now. Would you care to accompany us?"

"No, Bose and I will return to my ranch."

Little more than a week passed before another attempt to steal horses was made on the ranch, but this time it wasn't Navajos skulking in the night.

It was around two in the morning when the ruckus began. Jake was on guard at one corner of the corral that the men had built between the main house and the cowboys' soddies. Bose stood shivering at the opposite corner. Nearly at the same time, they noticed the horses begin to mill about the enclosure. There hadn't been any noises audible to the guards' ears, but something had the animals on the move. It had to be Indians.

Jake instinctively dropped to one knee. Bose stooped into a crouch as he crawled through the rails of the corral. Two horses were headed for the gate, and Jake could swear that they had ten feet between them, an extra pair in the middle. Carefully he aimed his rifle and squeezed off a round.

"Yi-i-ee-ee!" came a scream of pain.

The horses stampeded inside the fence with the sound of the shot, racing first to one corner, then another. Bose backed up against the railing, still crouching and with his rifle ready. The darkness was making it difficult for him to identify anything other than the horses.

"I think I hit one!" shouted Jake. Then his rifle discharged again. A Comanche brave had mounted the

fence behind him and then jumped down on the un-
suspecting cowboy, driving his knife deep into Jake's
shoulder. Jake lost the rifle and his hat as the weight of
the Indian crushed him against the ground. He rolled to
one side, but the Indian was on him instantly. A buck-
skinned knee drove hard into his stomach, forcing from
his lungs what little air was left. The Comanche, thinking
that he had already made the kill, grabbed Jake's hair and
drew his arm high over his head as he prepared to scalp
his victim. "Ai-ee—" the warrior began to cry in vic-
tory, but a blow to the side of his head cut him short.
Jake's hand had landed on a large rock, and he had
grabbed it instinctively for a weapon. Without hesitating
to think, he smashed the stone against the Indian's temple, knocking him senseless. The rock still in his hand,
Jake rolled over to the Indian, and although the tremen-
dous pain in his shoulder tried to deny him, he lifted the
rock high over his head and smashed his attacker's face
with it. Then the lack of air dropped him into total unconsciousness.

The second shot from Jake's gun had alerted the entire
ranch as to what was amiss. While Jake struggled for his
life, the rest of the cowboys poured out of their warm
huts to defend the property of their employers. Armed
with rifles and revolvers, they ran for the corral.

The Comanches, in the meantime, had begun to swarm
over the fence in pursuit of the horses. Some were on foot,
but most were mounted. One warrior leaped his pony
over the railing near Bose without seeing the black cowboy. Bose brought him down with the first shot, then
looked for another target. He fired again, killing a second
brave. One Comanche shouted something that sent his
comrades scurrying in all directions away from the corral.
Bose prepared to take his third shot, but before he could,
several shots came from the soddies. He flattened out on

the ground and rolled under the bottom rail of the fence. From a prone position, he fired at the fleeing Comanches. More shots rang out, and there were more shouts from the Indians as they rode away. A few were still trying to catch horses inside the corral. One got lucky and grabbed a mount, but his good fortune was short-lived as Bose's Henry spewed out a slug that toppled him to the dirt. Another buck went to his aid, but a shot from one of the cowboys racing up to the scene ended his life too. The last brave made an easy target as he climbed the fence attempting to escape. Several shots left his body draped over the top rail.

"One-armed" Billy Wilson nearly stepped on Bose when he came up the corral, firing at the retreating Comanches. At first, Billy thought Bose was an Indian, and he lowered his rifle to shoot the redskin.

"They're runnin' now," said a happy Bose, not realizing that Billy's gun barrel was only inches from his ear.

"Good God, it's you, Bose!" said Billy, startled by the fact that he had almost murdered a friend. He changed the aim of his weapon. "I thought you was an Injun. Darned near shot you. Good thing you spoke up when you did or I woulda killed you for certain."

Bose rolled over on his back to see Billy standing over him. He broke out laughing at the sight of the one cowboy who never let a deformed arm stop him from being and doing what he wanted. There he was, "One-armed" Billy Wilson, out in the middle of the night with nothing on but his long johns, boots, hat, and gunbelt. His rifle barrel rested on his crippled arm as he stared inquisitively down at Bose.

"What's so funny?" he asked.

Bose knew that the truth was something Billy didn't exactly want to hear at that particular moment, especially when one considered that Billy was reputed to possess one of the quickest and meanest tempers in all of Texas.

"Ain't nothin' funny, Billy. I'm just happy to be alive."

The fight was over. The Comanches were gone, and the horses were safe. The only cowboy to sustain an injury was Jake Tatum. He was fortunate that the Indian's knife had entered his shoulder on the outside of his shoulder blade, causing the point to tear up muscle only. The wound was packed with mud from the Pecos, and he was rushed off to Fort Sumner, where a doctor cleaned and dressed the injury properly. Jake would be two months healing.

Goodnight and Loving had been away when the Comanches struck the ranch. They had gone to Fort Bascom to complain about the stolen cattle being sold at Fort Sumner through a certain contractor. They had recognized some of the brands on the beeves and knew that the animals had come to New Mexico by way of the Comancheros, outlaw traders who dealt with the Comanches and other renegades. The Army promised to stop the traffic and to bring the brigands to justice. They were a long time in fulfilling their promises.

In the meantime, contracts had to be filled, and plans had to be made for the coming year's business.

The deal with the butchers in Santa Fe was becoming troublesome to the partners. It didn't bring the same profit that they were getting from the military, and the drives to the New Mexican capital were time-consuming. They agreed that the February delivery would be the last.

Loving always led the drive to Santa Fe, and he usually took the same four drovers with him: "One-armed" Billy Wilson, Frank Willborn, Jim Fowler, and Bose. It wasn't much of a drive, more a diversion away from the boredom of the ranch. The best thing about it was the overnight stay in Santa Fe. It gave Billy and Frank a chance to blow off a little steam, but Jim and Bose didn't need any such outlet. They went along primarily as guards, a precautionary measure for those times when Loving was carrying the money from the cattle sales.

On the last trip to Santa Fe, Loving suggested that he take a ride up to Denver after the delivery was made to the butchers. Spring was coming soon, and the partners would be in need of the money that he had deposited there the year before. Goodnight agreed to the detour.

When Jake Tatum heard about the plan, he talked Jim Fowler into letting him have his job on the drive. Loving wasn't sure that he liked the idea, but he permitted the change when Jake convinced him that he was completely healed.

Bose noticed a few changes in Denver that cold afternoon in February when they rode into the city. The construction that had been so prevalent the summer before had ceased because of the season, making the town appear to be sedate and settled. That was also attributable to the time of the year. The buildings that had been going up the previous summer were completed, and the streets lacked the crowded activity. Inside the warm hostelries, it was a different story. They were full of miners who had come down from the mountains to sit out the winter, most waiting for the snow, which blocked the passes and canyons, to melt away in the spring.

The Brown Hotel had the last available room in town. Loving insisted that the four cowboys share it with him, because their only alternative was to sleep in the loft over a livery stable. They agreed to stay if Loving would take the only bed in the ten-by-twelve lodging space.

Since there was no reason to retrieve the money until the following morning, there was ample time for recreation. Jake, Frank, and Billy hurried off to the friendly confines of a nearby saloon, but Bose wouldn't go anywhere until he had had his weekly bath. Loving waited for him, because he was afraid to leave the black cowboy on his own. The older man's fear was based on two things: Bose's age and his color. He was positive of the youth's abilities on the open range, but he wasn't so certain that Bose could cope with all the possible evils of a city the size of Denver.

Dressed in a clean plaid shirt and denim pants, Bose was ready to spend some of the money he had been saving for months. He walked with Loving over to the Belmont Saloon. The boss had a few short beers in mind and would maybe watch a poker game or two. The cowboy had but one thought: Hannah.

Unlike the summer before, the barroom was crowded, mostly with miners and with gamblers who were fleecing the miners out of what little gold they had brought down from the mountains with them. Nearly every table had a card game, usually stud or draw poker. Several men were gathered around the faro tables in the rear. A dozen or so women, each attired in brightly colored lace and silk gowns that revealed most of what men wanted to see, circulated about the hall, coaxing drinks from grasping customers and accepting invitations from others. Bose couldn't see Hannah among them, and this disappointed him. Loving spotted Jake and Frank at the bar. Billy was nowhere to be seen. The cowman picked his way through the boisterous throng to join Tatum and Willborn. Bose just naturally followed him.

"Y'all wanta try a beer again, Bose?" asked Jake. "It's cold this time of the year."

"Nope. I still think that stuff is bad."

"Then, how about a shot of whiskey?" asked Frank.

Bose shook his head. "Nope. That's worse yet. I'll just stand here and talk."

"Suit yourself," shrugged Jake. "Can't see how y'all gonna enjoy yourself just standin' here talkin'."

"Bose has other things on his mind," said Loving as he gave Jake a wink. "More important things than drinking with his friends."

"I see what you mean, Mr. Lovin'." Tatum turned to view the room, then noted that Bose was doing the same. "She ain't down here, Bose. Saw her earlier. She went up them stairs with some fella, but don't worry none. She'll be back."

A cloud came over Bose's face. "Who you talkin' about?"

Jake turned back to his drink. "Have it your way, pard. I was just tryin' to be helpful. Y'all just go ahead and have it your way."

"Jake was just trying to help, Bose," said Loving.

Bose put a hand on Jake's shoulder. "I know you mean well, Jake, but I kinda like to do this myself this time." He paused to let that sink into Jake, then added, "You really think she'll be comin' down soon?"

"Sure, Bose, she'll be down soon. Just wait and see."

Bose was more knowledgeable about Hannah's profession than he was when he had first met her. Without being too obvious, he had asked questions of the older cowboys about women like Hannah. He hadn't been too fond of the answers, but he learned to accept them, rationalizing that what a woman did before she settled down with one man was her business. His mother had always taught him to take people in this world for themselves. "Give each one a clean paper," she would say, "and let them mark it up for you." It was sound advice that he had always adhered to.

With his patience running out, Bose saw Hannah emerge from the hallway at the top of the stairs. The purple satin of her dress blended nicely with the creamy chocolate of her complexion. She was prettier than he remembered. His face gleamed with ivory as he watched her gracefully descend the staircase. Without saying another word to his companions, he left the bar to cut across the barroom floor to meet her at the bottom of the stairs. Hannah saw him coming. She didn't know whether to be happy or angry. On the one hand, she liked Bose, mostly because he was the same race she was. On the other, the goodness she saw in him made her dislike what she was. In spite of her feelings, she continued to descend.

"Hello, Hannah," he greeted her as she reached the last step.

"Well, if it ain't Mose from Texas," said Hannah as she went into the welcoming act that she used for most of her patrons.

"You got the place right, but the name is Bose. That's all right, though, because I can't expect you to recollect it since we barely knowed each other."

"Yes, Bose. How have you been? Would you like to buy me a drink?"

"Nope. I got other things on my mind."

She masked her face with a smile that Bose thought was affectionate. "Well, then, just follow me." She turned and headed back up the stairs with Bose fast at her heels. A few quick feet down the hall and they entered her room. "Well, now, have you changed your mind about all this?"

"Nope. I just come to talk."

Hannah frowned.

"I just wanted to see you again."

"Well, you have to pay—even for that," said Hannah, her hand held out in front of her, palm up.

"How much?" asked Bose as he dug into his pockets. "I got lots of money. See?" He showed her a few coins, all gold.

"This will do," she said as she picked out a ten-dollar piece. "Now, what do you want to talk about?"

"I want to know more about you," he said eagerly. He stuffed the other coins into his pockets. "I can recollect everythin' you said the last time, but I want to know more."

Hannah sighed, then flopped down on the bed. "You might as well sit down here beside me. I promise I won't bite." She patted the bed next to her, and Bose sat down. "There ain't no more to tell than what I already told you, so let's talk about you. Tell me more about that family of yours back in Texas."

Bose was delighted that she remembered. They talked away an hour before Hannah announced that she would have to go back to work downstairs. Bose was reluctant to let the session come to an end, as was Hannah. She really liked talking to him, and she especially enjoyed Bose because he treated her as though she was a person instead of a commodity. That was a rare experience for a woman in trade. Still, she knew her job and insisted on returning to the barroom.

"I got more money," said Bose, offering her another coin. "I can pay for more time."

"No, Bose, you keep your money." She reached out with one thin hand to touch his cheek. "You're a sweet man, and I really like you. You keep your money. You might need it someday for something better than me."

"There ain't nothin' better than you, Hannah."

She kissed him. "You really are sweet, Bose. If things were different, who knows what might have become of us? But they ain't different, so you keep your money and let me get back to work."

"Things could be different, Hannah," said Bose, a tinge of anxiety slipping into his voice.

"No, Bose, not now they can't." She opened the door and stepped into the hall. "Now, you go about your business and let me go about mine. Okay?"

Bose wasn't discouraged. He knew there would be another time. He watched her float away from him and down the stairs to the saloon to mingle with the customers. One grabbed her around the waist and pulled her down on his lap. Bose didn't like that. He raced down the steps and marched over to the table where Hannah was sitting, but before he could say or do anything, Jake slid in front of him.

"There you are, Bose," slurred Jake. "Mr. Lovin' says y'all is s'pose to get back to the hotel. He wants you there *muy pronto*, so you best get goin'."

"In a minute, Jake," said Bose as he started to push himself past his friend. "I got somethin' more important to do right now."

"No, you don't," insisted Jake, suddenly not as drunk as he had seemed. He put his hand on Bose's gun. "You can't do nothin' but get yourself invited to a necktie party if you keep on. You get my meanin'?"

Bose was quick to realize that his friend was right. "I guess I best get back to the hotel."

"That's right, pard. It's for the best."

Bose eased past Jake and made for the door. Jake watched him go to make sure he didn't turn back. Hannah saw him leave too. She hoped he would never come back. She would have made that wish into a prayer if a pinch from her customer hadn't caused her to shriek. Remembering her place, she grabbed the offending hand and playfully spanked it.

The last thing Bose heard as he left the Belmont was Hannah's laughter. It was haunting. As much as he wanted to go back and drag her away from that place, he knew there was nothing he could do, but he swore to himself that one day he would take her away from there.

SEVEN

The Pecos was running high the day the Goodnight-Loving outfit left the Bosque to return to Texas. The winter had been fairly mild and dry, and the spring of 1867 was drier than usual. That was in the low areas. In the mountains, it was just the opposite. The warm breezes up from the Gulf of Mexico had an early start at thawing the snow in higher elevation, thereby raising the river levels a tad above normal depths.

The partners thought it wise to travel the same route back that they had used to come to New Mexico. This decision was made in spite of the persistent reports of Comanches raiding everyone who used Horsehead Crossing. After all, they resolved, what they had heard were only rumors. Fact said if they took the direct course across the Plains, they would encounter more than Comanches. Kiowas and Apaches were also masters of the prairie.

Before leaving the Bosque, the remnants of the two herds that had been brought there the previous year had to be rounded up. Once that was done, the partners entrusted the beeves to Jim Foster, who, along with two other hands, trailed them north to the Capulin Vega, where they could be summered until Goodnight and Loving returned later that season.

Due to depredations of thieving Indians throughout the winter, the saddle and working stock of the ranch had dwindled to the point where some of the men were taking turns using the same horse on alternate days. Goodnight

scoured the countryside in search of more horses, but
since good cow ponies were still few and far between
those days in that part of New Mexico and since most
men weren't willing to part with a good saddle horse, he
was not able to find enough to go around. In fact, a couple of the wranglers were forced to ride mules all the way
to Texas. One of those cantankerous beasts presented
quite a problem along the way.

The few days it took the outfit to ride along the Pecos
from the Bosque to the vicinity of Horsehead Crossing
were uneventful. But as they approached the ford, Goodnight thought it expedient to scout the terrain ahead,
mostly to look for signs of Indians. He took one side of
the river, and Bose rode the other. The main body of cowboys lingered a few miles upstream until the scouts returned.

Goodnight was back first, reporting he hadn't seen any
signs of Indians. Then Bose came in.

"I done found a camp just south of the crossin'," he
said quickly. This was bad news. Goodnight and Loving
had hoped not to hear it. "Only seen about six ponies, but
there could be more. If that's all there is, they ain't gonna
bother us none."

"Let us hope that there are no more than that," said
Loving.

"There may be more elsewhere," said Goodnight. "We
might as well be prepared for the worst. Everyone have
your weapons ready for a fight just in case. Bose and I will
return to scouting. Oliver, you get the men moving and
try to keep Frank back with the rest of the men. There's
no need to take any extra risks."

"I'll stick close to him myself, Charlie," said the older
man. "Good luck; I'll see you at supper."

Frank Willborn was one of the misfortunate men in the
outfit. Instead of a good saddle horse, he had drawn a

mule, and to make matters worse, he had the stubbornest one in the lot. It was saddle-broken well enough, but it had a bad habit of wanting to lead. No matter how hard Frank pulled back on the reins, the animal went its own way and at its own pace.

"You had better keep a tighter rein on that mule," warned Loving as he rode up to where Frank was saddling his mount. "Bose reported seeing some Comanches up ahead."

"Aw, there ain't nothin' to worry about, Mr. Lovin'," said Frank with a casual grin. "There's too many of us for any bunch of Comanches to bother."

"That kind of thinking is liable to get you killed," said Loving. "Just the same, you stay back with the rest of us."

Frank really did try to keep the mule in the pack, but it was for nothing, as the beast took the lead right off. Loving was true to his word, as he rode alongside Frank all the way to the crossing. They left the rest of the cowboys and the chuck wagon a quarter mile behind.

"We had best wait here for the others," said Loving.

"I'd like to, Mr. Lovin', but this danged fool won't stop."

The mule plunged into the river, the water swirling around its knees. It drank as it waded across the ford. Loving permitted his horse to drink, but when he saw Frank's mount start up the opposite bank, he kicked his horse into action. By the time he was on the other side, Frank was topping the first hill. Loving spurred his mare into a gallop to climb the rise. When he reached the top, Frank was far down the back slope.

"Come back!" shouted Loving. He could see what Frank evidently hadn't. Six Comanche warriors were straight ahead of him. "Come back, Frank! Indians! There are Indians right in front of you!"

Frank didn't hear the warning, but he did hear the volley of rifle fire the Comanches let loose in his direction. He fought desperately to turn the mule, but the beast was oblivious to the danger as the bullets went whistling past. When one slug kicked up some sand near its feet, the animal took the hint, because it began to heed the constant pressure Frank was putting on the reins.

Loving drew his rifle from its saddle case, and he opened up on the Indians. The Comanches felt no danger from the cowman, as he was too far away for his bullets to do them much harm. The warriors ceased their shooting as they took to watching Frank and his mule parade in front of them. They must have thought him crazy, because they pointed at him and laughed. A sudden flurry of shots from the hill ended their merriment and drove them for cover.

"Let's go after them," said Billy Wilson. A chorus of similar requests was made by the other cowboys, who had come at a gallop when they heard the first sound of gunfire.

"No, let them be," said Loving. "We have ninety miles of desert ahead of us, and I don't want to waste our horses chasing a handful of Comanches." Loving let out a loud guffaw as he caught sight of Frank. "We have enough of a problem down there." He waved his rifle in Frank's direction.

The cowboys broke into laughter as they watched Willborn struggling to control his mount as the mule gave him a merry ride through the mesquite brush. He was whipping the animal with the reins at one second, then pounding it with fists the next. It brayed with every blow, complaining about the brutality. To add to the comedy, Frank was cussing every inch of the way with every swear word he could muster, even in Spanish. The mule made a full circle, eventually coming to halt at the top of the hill, where it had all begun. The stop was so sudden

and unexpected that Frank lurched forward from the saddle, grabbing the beast around the neck in order to keep
himself from being thrown completely off the animal.
Just as abruptly, the mule plopped itself down on its
haunches. Already dangling from the side of the mule's
head, Frank lost his grip and fell to the ground, landing
on his rump but still clutching the reins. There he was,
sitting in the dust, hat askew, surprise, then anger all over
his face. He started to curse the intransigent hinny, but a
roar of appreciative laughter from his friends cut him
short.

"What y'all funnin'?" he demanded. Before anyone
could answer, the mule joined in with a series of boisterous hee-haws. Frank thought about beating the animal,
but he kept his temper under control. "Danged fool animal! Y'all nearly got me killed!" Then he laughed, glad to
be alive.

Bose and Goodnight missed Frank's show. They heard
the shooting, but they did nothing about it because their
attention was focused on a much greater problem. They
found a larger encampment of Comanches in the hills
above Castle Canyon.

"Must be trouble back at the crossin'," said Bose as he
knelt on the ground next to Goodnight. They were watching the Indian camp from behind a large boulder. "Probably the other Comanch' I seen."

"This bunch must not have heard the shooting," said
Goodnight. "None of them are moving with any alarm."

"They're gonna know about it soon enough," said Bose.

A quizzical expression on his face, the cowman turned
to front Bose.

The black motioned with his head in the direction of
the river. "I think they're gonna tell all about it, and then
we're gonna have real trouble."

Goodnight knew Bose was speaking a truth he didn't

want to confront as he watched the six Comanches raising a cloud of dust. "We'd better wait and see what happens first. It's near sundown, and the dirty buggers might not want a fight just yet."

They watched as the warriors rode into the main camp. Initially, there was a great excitement as the Indians grabbed their mounts and weapons. Some started to ride out, but they quickly retreated when they saw their chiefs lingering. As the braves gathered around them, the leaders debated on strategy. When one pointed at the setting sun, Goodnight knew what they were up to.

"They will probably send out a few scouts to keep an eye on our outfit," said the cowman. "They can watch all they want. We won't be anywhere near here when the sun comes up tomorrow."

Goodnight moved to get on his horse, and Bose followed right behind him. They rode off to meet the rest of the outfit, which was just then approaching Castle Canyon.

"Hold them up there, Oliver," said Goodnight as he and Bose rode up. "There's a big war party waiting for us up ahead. From what I can tell, they aim to jump us at sunup. They will probably come straight through the pass with the sun at their backs. That will make it a hard fight for us."

"What do you suggest we do, Charlie?" asked Loving, knowing about Goodnight's experience as an Indian fighter.

"We will make camp as if we suspected nothing," said Goodnight. "After it becomes dark, we will pack everything and start moving again. I don't think the Comanches will attack us in the dark, and if luck is with us, we can ride through the canyon without them knowing about it till morning. By then, we should be miles away from here."

Few plans ever work as expected, but Goodnight's proved better than hoped. When the sun came up in their faces the next morning, the cowboys were fifteen miles into the Llano Estacado, the Staked Plains, and the Comanches were left to attack an empty camp. Three days later the cowboys were home.

Bose hadn't seen his family for over a year, and he asked permission from Loving to take a few days to visit his folks. Loving approved the request without reservation or hesitation. He knew Bose had celebrated his twentieth birthday just two months before, and he knew there was still a lot of boy left in the black cowboy.

Bose rode straight for Weatherford, heading for Shantytown, on the east side. There were some new buildings going up in the town, which was a good sign that prosperity was returning to Texas. He was glad of that. It meant his father was probably able to find work. Shantytown looked almost exactly as it had when he left it to go to work for Loving. Some of the shacks looked to be in better condition, and there were a few permanent homes to be seen. It was Shantytown just the same.

"Bose! Bose Ikard!" a familiar voice hailed him as he rode down the lane between two rows of rickety structures. "You is still alive!"

Bose turned to see Lukey Bowen, a childhood friend, running toward him. "Lukey!" he shouted back before jumping down from his horse. "You sure are a sight for these tired eyes!"

The two young men slapped their hands together in a warm handshake, then jostled each other with playful jabs and pushes.

"We done heard you was killed by Injuns last year," said Lukey. "Man, is your mammy gonna be surprised to see you! She done give you up for dead. I got to see the look on her face when she sees you comin' through the gate."

"My mammy ain't got no gate," said Bose, completely ignoring the rest of Lukey's words.

"She does now," reported Lukey. "And she got a fence to go with it."

"What kind of crazy talk is this, man?" asked Bose. "There ain't no one got no fence in Shantytown."

"Your mammy don't live in Shantytown no more," explained Lukey. "Your pappy done bought hisself a farm outside of town."

Bose grabbed Lukey by the arms. "You ain't lyin', now, are you, Lukey?"

"Man, just go see for yourself." Lukey pointed down the road. "It's straight ahead, about a mile or so. You can't miss it. It's the only one out there."

Bose looked down the road. He couldn't see anything that resembled a farm. "Take me to it, Lukey."

Lukey glanced at Bose's horse. "Do I have to walk?"

"Course not, man," Bose laughed. "You can ride up with me. I'll even let you have the saddle to ride on."

Lukey didn't wait to be told again. He leaped into the saddle, and then Bose jumped up behind him.

"I ain't rid no hoss in a long time," confessed Lukey.

"Well, don't tell the hoss," said Bose. "Just pretend you know what you're doin' up here."

"I don't need to pretend, Bose Ikard. You just hold on and watch me."

Lukey kicked the horse in the ribs with the heels of his bare feet, and they were off at a gallop. A few minutes later he pulled back on the reins to halt the animal in front of a small white frame house with a white picket fence around it.

"Miz Ikard!" shouted Lukey. "You come on out here, Miz Ikard! I got somethin' special for you to see." Bose slid down off the horse's rump and walked over to the gate to wait for his mother to come from the house. Lukey leaned over and said secretly to Bose, "I'm gonna fetch your pappy from the field."

As Lukey rode away, Bose heard some grumbling coming from within the house. It was his mother complaining about Lukey disturbing her in the middle of preparing the noon meal for her husband. Bose couldn't understand much of what she was saying, but when she opened the door, he heard her perfectly.

"Now, what you got that's so special, Lukey Bowen?"

Sheba Ikard stepped through the door onto the porch. The bright light of day blinded her for a moment as she took the few steps down the path to the gate. Halfway to the fence, she shaded her eyes with one fleshy hand.

"Well, out with it, boy. What you—" She stopped, frozen still. "Oh, Lordy, it's a ghost!" She backed away a pace.

Bose pushed the gate open. "No, Mammy, I ain't no ghost." He stepped into the yard. "Injuns ain't got your Bose yet."

"Bose!" she cried. Tears burst from her eyes. "My baby, my baby's home!" She dashed to embrace her son. "You is home, son. My baby's home."

Bose squeezed his mother to him as she kissed his face in a dozen places with two dozen kisses that seemed to come all at once.

"Yes'm, Mammy, I'm home; I'm home."

Sheba pushed herself free of his arms. "Lemme look at you, son." She appraised him quickly. "You sure is a fine-lookin' man. Just like your pappy." She hugged him again. "Come on. We got to find your pappy right now."

Bose stopped her. "Lukey done gone to fetch him on my hoss. He'll be here soon." He looked at the house. "Besides, I want to see this here new home."

Sheba took Bose by the hand and pulled him toward the door. "Just you wait and see what your pappy done got for me. This house's almost as nice as the one Massa Ben done had back in Mississipp'." She went through the doorway ahead of Bose. "Take a look. Ain't it somethin'?"

The first thing Bose noticed was the floor. It was wood instead of dirt. Then he saw chairs and a sofa, a real sofa, all covered with cloth just like white folks had. A stone fireplace dominated one wall, and on the mantel was a photograph of his parents. He walked over to it to inspect it more closely. They were standing in front of the house, dressed in their Sunday meeting clothes and the pride they felt in their new home was in their eyes if not on their lips.

"Come on. Lemme show you the kitchen." Sheba pulled him into the room, where food was cooking on a new iron stove. The table was cluttered with potato peelings, a bowl of peeled potatoes, and a knife. "See. We got a pump in here too. Don't gotta run outside in the cold no more to get in fresh water."

Bose touched the handle of the water pump. "This is really somethin', Mammy. Where'd Pappy get all the money to buy this place?"

The sound of the front door opening and slamming shut stopped his mother from answering.

"Sheba!" shouted Amos Ikard as he passed through the living room. "Sheba, is you all right? Lukey Bowen say there's a stranger here." He entered the kitchen, his eyes wide with excitement. He saw Sheba first, her face glowing with the happiness only a mother can know. Then he saw Bose. He failed to recognize his son at first glance, because his eyes were slow to adjust to the dimmer light of the house. As soon as he recognized his son, he wasted no time expressing himself. "Bose." He said the name as if it was holy, then he embraced his only child.

"It's me, Pappy," said Bose as he returned his father's affection.

"Praise the Lord!" cried Amos. Happy tears poured down his cheeks. "You done come back after all." He held Bose at arm's length to get a better look at the man who had left his home as a boy. "You're a real man, son, a real man."

Sheba moved closer to her man. "He still my little Bose." She put her hand to Bose's face. "Ain't nothin' never gonna change that."

"We done heard you got killed by the Comanch'," said Amos.

"Come close a time or two," said Bose, "but they ain't got me yet."

"Come sit here, and tell us all about where you been and what you been doin'," said Amos as he slid a chair out from under the table.

Sheba put her large body on another, the folds of her girth swallowing the wooden seat. She resumed the chore of peeling potatoes while she listened to Bose recount his tales of the trail and the men he shared them with. The storytelling lasted throughout the remainder of the morning and through the noon meal.

"Now," said Bose to his father when he was finished with his narrative, "I want to know how you got this place. Where'd the money come from, Pappy?"

"Ain't it wonderful," said Sheba. "Tell Bose all about it, Pappy."

"Well, it was like this. This man come down to Shantytown one day last summer."

"It was spring," interjected Sheba.

"That's right, spring," agreed Amos. "This man got all the men to gather round him, and then he started tellin' us we got rights. He say we can own our own land and farm it if we want to. We ask the man how we gonna do

that when there ain't none of us got no money. Then he
say that ain't no problem. He hold up a bunch of money
in his fist and say he got the money. What he needs is
men who want to own their own farm and who want to
farm it. All we got to do is put our mark on this here piece
of paper he had. Then he give us the money to buy a
farm. Then he take us to the bank, and the banker man
sell us a farm."

"Who had this farm before you got it?" asked Bose.

"White folks," said Amos. "The man's name was Clark.
He got himself killed fightin' in the war. His widow done
moved away because she couldn't pay the taxes. The
money I paid was for the taxes. Now the farm is mine."

"What did this paper you put your mark on say?"
asked Bose.

"The man say that it say I borrow the money from him
and that I got to pay it back."

"How do you got to pay it back?"

Amos leaned back in his chair. "You sure is full of questions, son."

"How do you got to pay it back?" insisted Bose.

"The man say I pay back fifty dollars a year till it's paid
back."

"How many years do you got to pay?"

Amos furrowed his brow, a quizzical expression domi-
nating his face. "I don't rightly know. Can't recollect that
part of the deal."

"Who is this man?" asked Bose.

"Name is Krantz," said Amos. "He come here from a
place he call Pennsylvany. That's a Yankee state up
North."

"This here Krantz; is he a white man?"

"No, he's a nigger like us," said Amos.

"Where'd a nigger like us get all that money?" asked
Bose, already more than suspicious.

Amos was puzzled. "Don't know that it's any of my business. All I know is that he got it and he loaned it to me. Then I buy me a farm."

"Uh-huh," nodded Bose.

"How come you're so suspicious, Bose?" asked Sheba.

"Mammy, I've been hearin' all sorts of stories where men come down here from the North doin' all sorts of nice things for us poor black folks."

"What's wrong with that?" she retorted.

"For one thing, Mammy, the white folks down here don't like it. The white folks is sufferin' somethin' fierce because they lost the war to these nice men from up North. They're takin' homes from all kinds of folks, then sellin' them to black folks just like Pappy. Now, they ain't doin' that just because they're nice folks. They got to be makin' money on this somehow."

"That why you ask how many years I got to pay back the money?" asked Amos.

"That's right, Pappy," said Bose. "You gonna have the money to pay back this man?"

"I will when I harvest my crops," said Amos.

"How are you gonna live till then?" inquired Bose.

"We got credit down at the store in town," smiled Sheba. "We can get 'most anythin' down there. I just tell the man to put it on our 'count."

"Is that so?" Bose scratched his head, then rubbed the back of his neck. "It don't all sound right to me, Pappy. Got to be a catch to this someplace. I don't reckon what it is yet, but I'm sure gonna find out. There's got to be somethin' wrong with all this."

Amos and Sheba were silent. They couldn't see what was wrong or if anything was wrong at all with borrowing money to buy a farm. All they knew was they had their very own place and no one was going to take it away from them.

"Did this man, Krantz, give you any paper for this farm, Pappy?" asked Bose.

Amos' eyes lit up. "He sure did. Mammy, where is that paper?"

"I keep it safe under the bed," she answered without moving.

Amos wrinkled his brow. "Well, don't just sit there, woman. Go and fetch it here."

Sheba pushed her heavy frame out of her seat and waddled away toward the bedroom. A moment later, she was back in the kitchen with a piece of folded parchment. Amos reached for it, but Bose's hand got there first. He unfolded the stiff paper, glancing over it as if he were reading every word inscribed on its rough surface.

"Where you learn to read?" asked Amos.

Bose rolled his eyes. "I didn't."

"Uh-huh," mocked his father.

"This here paper looks all right," said Bose. "It got a seal and all, but I still don't know. Pappy, I want to take this to Mr. Lovin' and have him read it. He knows the law, and he'd know if this is legal or not."

"You do that, son," said Sheba. "Have Mr. Lovin' read it and make sure it's all legal and proper."

Bose nodded.

The next day, he was standing in front of Loving, who was sitting in an overstuffed leather armchair in the living room of his ranch house. The cowman let the parchment rest on his lap. Bose fidgeted with his hat, rolling the brim between nervous fingers.

"Well, what does it say, Mr. Lovin'?" asked Bose.

"This is a legal document, Bose. This man, Krantz, knew exactly what he was doing when he had your father make his mark on it." Loving tilted his head forward, glancing down at the paper before him. "It says your father is over a barrel."

"I don't understand, Mr. Lovin'. How does this Krantz got Pappy over a barrel?"

"Well, Bose, it's like this. Krantz loaned your father the money to buy his farm. Three hundred dollars, to be exact. Your father has to repay that money and the interest that goes with it. He has to pay Krantz fifty dollars a year for ten years. Now, that isn't bad. In fact, it's downright decent. Where he has your father over a barrel is this part in here about his credit at the store. It seems that Krantz owns the store. Your father has to settle accounts with the store before he makes his payment on the farm. The interest on his store account is very high. By the time your father gets through paying off his account each year, he isn't going to have much money left over. Maybe not even enough to make his farm payment. It all depends on how much he gets for his crops. If your father has a bad year with his crops, he will have to borrow more money from Krantz and go further into debt than he already is or lose his farm. It does not look very promising for your father."

Bose was silent as he tried to digest everything Loving had just disclosed to him. He shifted his weight from one foot to the other. He quit rolling his hat, dropping it to one side in his hand.

"It ain't fair, is it, Mr. Lovin'?"

"No, Bose, it isn't," sighed Loving, "but there is nothing your father can do about it if he wants to keep his farm."

Bose nodded stiffly. He reached for the document, and Loving handed it up to him. He stuffed it into a coat pocket without folding it. With downcast eyes, his head jerked spasmodically up and down. Dejection distorted the other features of his face as he backed away on rigid legs.

"Now, don't take it hard, Bose," consoled Loving as he

pulled himself out of the chair. "I'm sure your father and mother can make a go out of that farm. All indications so far are for a good year. The weather has been good for farming, and it looks like it will continue to be so. It will all turn out for the good. Just wait and see." He put a gentle hand on Bose's shoulder. "Put your faith in the Lord, Bose. I'm certain your parents are."

"Yessir, Mr. Lovin'." Bose turned to leave. "I guess you're right. My pappy is a hard-workin' man. He and Mammy can make it. They're good folks, and the Lord looks after good folks."

"That's right, Bose," said Loving as he walked the black cowboy to the door. "Don't worry yourself over this. We have another drive ahead of us to worry about."

"Yessir, Mr. Lovin'."

The boss patted him on the back, and Bose left.

At the end of the day, Bose rode back to his parents' home. He tied his horse to the picket fence. The gate squeaked when he opened and closed it. His mother met him at the door.

"You're just in time for supper, son," she said as she hugged him. "I done fixed up a mess of fresh dandelion greens to go with the jackrabbit your pappy kilt in the field this mornin'."

"That sounds real good, Mammy," said Bose, trying to display some enthusiasm but falling short. "Where's Pappy?"

"In here, Bose," Amos Ikard called from the kitchen. "Come on in here and sit yourself." Sheba and her son entered the kitchen. "Mammy, fix up Bose with a plate and fork. Sit down, son, and have some supper."

"Sure thing, Pappy," said Bose as he seated himself at the table. Then he noticed that he had forgotten to take off his coat. He slid his chair away from the table. His father's loan agreement crinkled noticeably in the pocket when he removed the jacket. He took the paper from the pocket and put it down next to his plate.

"Oh, yeah," said Amos. "What did Mr. Lovin' say about this?" He picked up the document.

Reluctantly, Bose repeated his employer's report. Neither Amos nor Sheba interrupted his narrative, which he finished with a heavy sigh.

"Is that all?" asked Amos after a moment of silence when Bose was through.

"Yessir, Pap," said his son, perplexed because his father seemed to be taking it very lightly.

"Well, I already knowed all that," said Amos as he reached for a piece of rabbit.

"That's right, son," reiterated Sheba. "Pappy and me done talked all about that before he buy this here farm. We knowed it was gonna take a heap of work to make it go."

"That's right," confirmed Amos, "and we knowed that Krantz was tryin' to rob us with that 'count at the store. I maybe can't read and write, but I sure do know my numbers. There ain't no man can out-figure Amos Ikard when it comes to money."

Bose was astounded. He couldn't comprehend how his father had become so smart since the last time they had been together.

EIGHT

The sign—those indications of the future that Nature provides for the almanac compiler—wasn't good that spring of 1867. For the farmer, it was just fine. The weather was warm enough, and the skies dropped an ample amount of moisture to ensure a good growing season. The birds had plenty of insects to feed on, and there were enough wild roots and grasses to keep the jackrabbits and cottontails away from devouring the family vegetable gardens. The men of the soil had no quarrel with Mother Nature that year.

The cattlemen had different ideas about the meteorological omens they were witnessing. Fair temperatures and a wet April and May were all right, because they meant plenty of grass for their stock to fatten up on, both before the roundups and during the drives that were to follow. But when the skies failed to clear in June, it was a dubious portent for the trail. Thunder and lightning weren't conducive to taming a herd en route to the railheads of Kansas or, in the Goodnight-Loving outfit's case, the ranges of New Mexico and Colorado.

There was another difficulty the ranchers faced that seldom troubled the farmers. A new leader had come to the fore among the bands of the Comanches. His mother had been a mere girl of ten when the Cossacks of the Plains swept down on her parents' farm, murdering the rest of her family and carrying her off into captivity. Cynthia Ann Parker was then raised as a Comanche, later

to become the wife of a chief and to bear him a son
and a daughter. When her husband was killed by Texas
Rangers, the lawmen returned her to her parents' people.
They didn't like the idea of her bringing her infant
daughter with her. They were almost relieved when the
child died. Cynthia Ann, who had not wanted to leave
the Comanches in the first place, tried to return to the
people she thought of as her own. She was forced to
remain with her white relatives. The anguish of a
different captivity was too much for her. She passed away
a young woman, from malnutrition, a self-imposed death
brought on by a broken heart.

Quanah, the son she had left behind, swore vengeance
on his white brothers when he learned of his mother's
death and the way she died.

By 1867, Quanah Parker had earned the respect of his
fellow warriors through deeds of prowess in battle. His
warbonnet had gained new eagle feathers with each fight
until he was recognized as the one war chief who could
stop the advance of the white man's civilization. From the
Panhandle to the Great Bend of the Rio Grande, Quanah
Parker was ready to seek retribution for his personal loss.

In spite of the sign, Goodnight and Loving went ahead
with their plans to take another herd to Colorado. They
hired back most of the men who had been with them the
year before, but each partner maintained his own crew.
They gathered two separate herds and agreed to combine
them for the drive. Loving's men worked the country
around Palo Pinto, while Goodnight's moved his cattle
and those he had legal powers to handle to Cribb's Sta-
tion. There the steers were branded with the circle road
mark and held under herd until the day to begin trailing
them.

The appointed day arrived for the outfit to break trail
for Colorado. For two days, everything was peaceful

enough, going much as expected. The cattle, nearly all steers this time, were taming down without too many mavericks running off. Tested by the experience of the previous year, the cowboys renewed their skills as they settled into their daily routine. Thirty miles were covered without incident.

A campsite near Camp Cooper, on the Clear Fork, was selected for the second night on the trail. Four men slowly circled the herd, making sure the beeves stayed in one place. The nightriders were far enough apart that they couldn't hear the man closest to them as each sang a lonesome song of the prairie. Bose intoned a spiritual his mother had taught him when he was a boy. Frank cracked out a drinking song, singing it soft and slow as he improvised a gentler melody for it. Jake yearned for a girl with yellow hair, and Jim Fowler cut loose an old slave working tune, which he had sung on a plantation in Louisiana. None of the four heard the Comanche war party until the Indians were in the midst of the cattle.

A single gunshot signaled the red raiders into yelling their war cries as they stampeded the herd in every direction at once. The night was so dark that it was impossible to tell one rider from the next at a distance of ten feet or more. Both sides held their fire for fear they might kill a comrade by accident.

"Injuns!" the cry went up as the entire camp was alerted to the threat. The cowboys jumped into their boots and saddles. Goodnight was the first on the ready as Bose rode into camp.

"How many are there?" asked the cattleman.

"Can't rightly tell," replied Bose. "They seem to be all over at once."

"What about the herd?" quizzed the cowman.

"They're goin' all ways at once, Mr. Goodnight," said Bose. "The Comanch' scattered them good."

"Damn!" swore Goodnight as he beat a fist against his holster. He drew his gun and turned to the other riders behind him. "Come on, boys, let's get after them."

"Won't do no good, Mr. Goodnight," said Jake as he came in at a gallop. "Those redskins already skipped off in the dark, and we got longhorns spread out all over the country."

"Damn!" swore Goodnight again.

"Take it easy, Charlie," cautioned Loving as he walked up to his partner. "It won't do any good to get yourself worked up. The best thing we can do right now is round up what we can, then wait for sunup to look for the rest."

Goodnight shoved his six-shooter back into its resting-place. "I suppose you're right, Oliver. Okay, boys, you heard the man. Let's get to it."

They were out only an hour before Goodnight called off the search. Most of the steers had remained close to the camp, and these were easily regrouped. The number of nightriders was doubled to safeguard against another incursion by the Comanches.

With the first light of day, Goodnight mounted up half the crew to go in search of the marauders. The rest of the men busied themselves with chasing down the few head that were still straying. Goodnight's party tracked the Indians to the brush along Clear Fork Bottom. They kept far back from there, because the cowman anticipated an ambush. Instead of forcing a confrontation, they returned to the camp.

"We found them," Goodnight reported to Loving. "I figure they'll hole up in the brush for the day and attack us again tonight. We had best find some decent place to camp tonight, a place we can easily defend. There's a valley near here where you can take the herd and bed them. I'll take Jim with me, and we will keep an eye on the Comanches. We'll rejoin you after dark if all goes well."

Loving found the valley Goodnight mentioned. He directed Jake and Billy Wilson to head the cattle to the far end along a ravine with steep banks. Otis Kinney set up his chuck wagon next to the gully, and Loving had Bose graze the horse remuda between the camp and the herd. Before the last bit of cerise sky faded into darkness, a double guard was posted on the perimeter of the circled longhorns. The outriders maintained their vigilance as alertly as their fatigue would allow. Only the arrival of Goodnight and Jim Fowler broke the monotony of the night.

Loving and Otis Kinney were sitting next to the campfire, warming themselves and drinking coffee, as Goodnight came galloping into camp. He leaped from his horse and dashed up to the fire. He grabbed the tin coffeepot and poured its contents over the flames. Not every ember was extinguished, so he stomped out the rest with his boots.

"Charlie, have you gone loco?" demanded a surprised Loving as he jerked on his partner's arm.

Goodnight shook himself free of the older man's grasp. "I sure haven't, but I have my doubts about your sanity. Don't you know this fire can be easily seen for miles? The Comanches couldn't ask for a better guide to this camp."

Loving was irritated at first, but then he saw that Goodnight was correct in his accusation.

"My apologies, Charlie," said the older man. "I thought we were safe here."

Goodnight heaved a heavy sigh. "No harm done, Oliver. Please forgive me for jumping at you like that. I had—"

"Like you said," Loving interrupted, "no harm done."

Goodnight stared down at the dead coals. "Suddenly, I wish I had a cup of that coffee."

"Here, take mine," offered Otis. He handed his nearly

full cup to the cowman, who didn't hesitate to accept it.

"Thank you, Otis."

"You look all worn out, Mr. Goodnight," said Otis.

"You do at that, Charlie," concurred Loving. "Maybe you should get some sleep. I'll wake you if anything happens."

"Well, just for an hour or so," demurred Goodnight. He finished the coffee with a deep gulp. "Just for an hour, mind you."

Loving nodded his agreement, and the younger man spread out a buffalo robe on the grass next to the chuck wagon. He was asleep as soon as he closed his eyes. Contrary to his orders, he wasn't awakened an hour later.

The expected attack came the hour before sunrise. The men sleeping in camp didn't know what was happening until they heard the first shots fired by the outriders at the mounted Comanches who were trying to stampede the herd. As the camp came to life, the men there were surprised by a second war party, which had gotten close to the chuck wagon by crawling along the gully. A third group seemed to come out of the ether as they went for the remuda. It was a well-planned assault.

On the perimeter of the herd, Bose and Jake rallied the guards while they awaited reinforcements from the camp. Jim Fowler and Frank Willborn joined them immediately.

"We got to fight," said Bose as he pulled his Colt. "The cattle can wait for now."

"It's too dark to see anything just yet," argued Jake.

"That's the chance we got to take," retorted Bose.

The others drew their weapons, and the four of them rode off toward the sounds of war cries. Bose fired at the first rider he saw. The man, Indian or white, kept going, but the reverberation of the shot roused the longhorns into moving. A second blast at another rider had them running.

"Now y'all done it," yelled Jake over the thunder of a few thousand hooves. "Dumb nigger, we'll have cows from here to the Pecos by sunup!"

"Bose, over there!" shouted Frank.

By instinct, Bose knew where Frank was pointing even though he couldn't see whatever it was Willborn was indicating. The black cowboy turned to see four Comanche warriors chasing steers away from the mainstream of the stampede. He fired the three rounds that were left in his pistol. One brave toppled from his pony and was trampled by the cattle he was trying to steal. The dying man's screams warned his comrades to take flight.

"Get them steers," ordered Bose.

Jim and Frank rode to turn back the leaders, while Bose and Jake went to join Billy Wilson, who was trying to head off the main body.

Goodnight awakened with the first shots. His immediate reaction was to reach for a weapon, but a shower of arrows kept him low to the ground, preventing him from getting to the guns he had left on his horse. The buffalo robe he had been sleeping on was turned up on one side. It acted as a shield against the deadly shafts the Indians in the gully were sending his way. The tough hide deflected every point into the ground, thus saving the cowman from injury.

Crouched behind a rear wheel of the chuck wagon, Otis Kinney opened up a steady fire on the raiders in the ravine. When Goodnight saw this, he made a dash for his horse. He would have joined Kinney in the defense of the camp, but a party of mounted Comanches drew his attention to the remuda. Quickly, he strapped on his gun belt and leaped into the saddle. Two flicks of the quirt sent the mare galloping to intercept the horse thieves.

Loving and the other men in the camp joined in the attempt to stop the stampeding herd. The overcast sky was becoming lighter, permitting the cowboys to see the dark mass they were trying to hold in check. They rode around the edges, constantly heading the steers in a counterclockwise direction.

The Indians continued to disrupt the efforts of the white men by riding into the herd, breaking off small bunches of cattle, and driving them away from the main body. Occasionally, a warrior would let loose with an arrow at whatever cowboy was close at hand. The shafts had little accuracy, coming from the bows of mounted archers shooting at moving targets. Only one wrangler suffered a hit. "Long" Joe Loving, a young man of the same name but unrelated to Goodnight's partner, was spilled from his saddle when he caught an arrow in his neck behind the left ear and at the base of his skull.

Goodnight was joined by Billy Taylor, a black youth who had joined the outfit that spring. The two of them charged the Comanches who were after the remuda. Surprised by the bold onslaught, the raiders veered away as they sought to circumvent the horse herd and take it from another side. Goodnight and Taylor proved to be superior horsemen, as they maintained a defendable position between the Indians and the horses.

As the gray skies lightened, the cowboys became more organized and the Comanches withdrew. A majority of the cattle were still together; the remuda was still intact; and Otis Kinney had protected the chuck wagon. The only casualty was "Long" Joe Loving. He wasn't dead, but he was in great pain when Jake brought him in to the chuck wagon, the arrow sticking out from his neck.

"Looks real nasty to me," said Jake as he helped Joe to the ground. "Don't see how y'all lived with that thing stuck in you like that."

"I'm a dead man right now," lamented Joe hoarsely.

"Not yet, you're not," said Goodnight as he inspected the wound.

"I got to be," argued Joe. "Knowed a feller once named Odie Cleaver what took an arrow in the exact same place. He ain't around no more to talk about it."

"Odie Cleaver never rode with me," countered Goodnight. He studied the shaft, noting that the point was made of hoop iron. If it had been steel or stone, the danger would have been minimal, because the shaft could be broken off and Joe could be sent back to the settlements, where a doctor could remove the point. As it was, the hoop iron would begin corroding immediately, leading to an infection that would eventually kill the young cowboy. The obverse of that was equally perilous. The arrowhead was imbedded in Joe's skull. To remove it with the rough hands and crude tools available on the open range might cause a fracture that could kill him in a second or in a week.

"Well, Joe," said Goodnight, sympathetic to the man's dilemma, "if I leave it in, you're going to die for certain. If I try to pull it out, I might kill you myself."

"But you might not either," said Joe. He sat calmly on the ground, his legs crossed as he contemplated his situation. Blood still trickled from the injury, running down his neck and back to be absorbed by his shirt. Perspiration had already saturated the garment, and more beaded up and dripped off him with each passing moment. He closed his eyes as a prayer dominated his thoughts, deluding the pain that coursed around his head and shoulders.

"You might be needin' these," said Otis as he handed Goodnight a pair of old-fashioned horseshoe pinchers.

By that time, nearly every hand in the outfit was gathered around Goodnight and Joe. The empathy they felt for both men was plain on their faces as they silently awaited the decision which had to be made soon.

Joe opened his eyes, and without moving his head, looked up to see the pinchers in Goodnight's hand. Panic twisted his features as his orbs bulged then shrank into blank terror.

"Get a good hold on him," said Goodnight.

Jake and Bose took Joe by the arms. Deftly, they turned him over and laid him face down between them. Each man put a knee against his shoulder blades as Billy Wilson straddled his legs, then sat on them. Oliver Loving knelt down at Joe's head, taking a firm grip on it above the ears. Goodnight took the shaft in his left hand as he fixed the pinchers onto the base of the arrowhead. He tightened his hold and gave a tug on the point. It didn't budge. He released the shaft and put both hands on the gripping tool.

"Let it all go, Joe," said Goodnight. "This isn't going to come easy."

He planted his feet and started a steady pulling. Joe screamed his agony to the horror of everyone watching the scene. The four men assisting Goodnight strained to sustain their holds on the man as Goodnight used every ounce of strength in his arms and shoulders to wrench the point out of the wound. All at the same time when the arrow came free, Goodnight stumbled backward; Jake and Bose lost their balance, bumping each other; and Joe ceased his terrible screams as he passed into unconsciousness.

"He's still alive," said Mr. Loving. "Otis, get this hole patched and get him into the wagon."

Kinney bandaged the wound, and Joe was laid in the chuck wagon. He was breathing steadily but had yet to regain consciousness.

"I'll keep an eye on him," volunteered Kinney.

"And the rest of us better get to rounding up the herd," said Goodnight.

The outfit spent the remainder of the day getting the steers back into some semblance of a herd. When they were finished, a count was taken whereby they discovered that six hundred head were missing. The partners reasoned that they should accept their loss and get the remainder moving again as soon as possible. A third raid by Quanah and his warriors could be expected again that night. As soon as the outfit ate and the last bit of daylight was gone, Loving gave the order to start driving the beeves out of the valley.

It was around midnight when the horizon ahead of them was etched with silver flashes. Distant peals of thunder lumbered across the prairie, warning the cowboys that a storm was surely coming their way. With each passing minute, the jagged bolts became more distinctive as they ripped through the clouds to the land below. The wind gained velocity. The scent of rain was in the air.

Before the first drops could come pelting down, the cowboys pulled on their slickers. The cattle bawled out their apprehension as each man expected them to stampede at any moment.

Suddenly, the wind ceased to howl. The lightning quit rattling the clouds. And strangely, the cattle went mute. Only the soft padding of their hooves on the spongy prairie wafted through the air.

The lull failed to last, as the storm broke upon them, cattle and cowboys, with intense ferocity. The leaders bolted from the herd. The steers immediately behind them picked up the pace, but the four men riding point were quick to react.

Billy Wilson, with Frank Willborn behind him, was on the left. Bose and Jake were to the right, gently edging the leaders toward Billy and Frank. Gradually, they let Bose and Jake turn the herd as they dropped back along one side. Within minutes, the stampede was curtailed, but the calm didn't last.

Lightning laced down from the clouds into the midst of the beeves. The booming flash stunned the steers in the nucleus into a standstill, but those on the perimeter broke in all directions at once. Every man went into action to halt the crazed animals.

The electric bolts continued to explode from cloud to cloud but stopped striking the earth. The rain became torrential, darkening the night even more. It was impossible for the cowboys to see anything that wasn't within a few feet of them. Only the bawling of the cattle and pounding of their hooves made the wranglers aware of the location of the herd.

"We can't stop them in this rain," Goodnight shouted over the roar of the storm to Loving as the two worked side by side. "We'll have to let them have their way."

With that, the cowmen rode off to tell the others. It took them a few minutes to call off most of the men, who then gathered around the chuck wagon to wait for daylight.

The cattle continued to run, but in an odd manner. Only those steers on the outer edges were actually stampeding. Those in the center walked along at their normal trail pace. Something or someone was preventing them from fractioning, driving them in a counterclockwise movement. The wranglers around the chuck wagon watched the scene in amazement.

"Hey, looky there!" shouted Jake, pointing to two glowing balls bouncing along on the horizon beyond the herd. "There's someone out there yet."

They were witnessing one of the phenomena of the plains. Some called it "Devil's fire," while others knew it for what it really was: static electricity. For some unknown reason, horses collected the energy during a storm, and it often caused an eerie sphere to glow between the animal's ears.

"I don't see Bose anywhere," said Frank. "Must be him out there."

"Billy Taylor ain't here neither," said Jake. "Them dumb niggers is crazy to be out there tryin' to stop that herd all by themselves."

They might have been out of their minds, but Bose and Billy succeeded in turning the leaders, making them run around the greater part of the mass of beef. The two blacks continued to force the cattle to circle for an hour, enough time to wear them down to a slow trot. It was nearly light when they finally stopped.

"I've got to thank you, Bose," said Loving after the partners had finished counting the herd later that morning. "You and Billy saved most of the herd. We only lost two hundred head last night."

Two days later, the outfit reached the Pecos. The herd, worn out from stampeding, was finally broken to the trail. The cowboys moved them up the Pecos Valley from Horsehead Crossing for nearly a hundred miles without incident and without seeing any sign of Indians. They were still south of the Guadalupe Mountains when Goodnight decided they should halt the drive for a full day in order to rest and recoup.

"We have already lost a great deal of time," argued Loving. He and Goodnight sat to one side of the campfire discussing the matter of the letting of contracts in Santa Fe. Billy Wilson, Jake Tatum, and Bose Ikard sat across from them, listening, only entering the conversation when spoken to. "The month is nearly over, and Santa Fe is still a long way off."

"What do you suggest, Oliver?" asked Goodnight.

"I will ride ahead to Santa Fe," he said bluntly.

"Alone? You can't do that," insisted Goodnight.

"Then I will take Bose with me," countered Loving.

Goodnight rolled his head to one side as he pondered the idea. He wasn't in favor of it. He knew there could be Indians lurking at every bend of the Pecos, just waiting to ride down on any white man who might come their way.

"If you ride by night," said Goodnight, "and hole up by day, it might be safe enough. I can't say that I like the idea, but I can see that your mind is made." He glanced over at Bose. "Instead of Bose, I think you should take Billy."

"I think I should go," said Bose, interjecting his own feelings into the talk.

Loving was surprised by the outburst. "I agree," he said. "Bose is my man."

"Maybe so," countered Goodnight, "but he's young and doesn't have the experience on the trail that Billy has. I know Bose can handle himself well enough in a fight, but Billy knows Indians."

"Yes, I see your point," said Loving. His eyes shifted to Bose, then back to Goodnight. "Bose should stay here with the herd."

"I still think I should go with you, Mr. Lovin'," insisted Bose. "It's just a feelin', but I—"

"Sorry, Bose," interrupted Goodnight. "The decision is made. I need you here, and Billy goes with Mr. Loving. You can leave tonight, Oliver."

Bose wanted to continue the argument, but he knew it would be of no value. He went to his bedroll that night with an intuition that disaster lay just ahead.

NINE

The trail north was easier than the miles the outfit traveled across the Texas desert. The cattle settled into a steady pace, made more manageable by their decreased numbers. The cowboys were satisfied that the worst was over, and Goodnight, although disappointed by the losses, was certain that there would be no further depredations by Quanah and his band of warriors.

Oliver Loving and Billy Wilson had been gone from the drive for three days when Bose, scouting in Goodnight's stead, spotted another outfit on the trail ahead. He was leery of making contact, because they appeared to be entirely Mexicans, which suggested Comancheros to him. As soon as he saw a white man giving orders, he felt it was safe to approach them. But, before he could, a lariat ringed him about the chest and shoulders. He held tight to the reins and squeezed his knees against the ribs of his horse. The jerk on the line came, the horse reared, and Bose fell to the ground. With catlike grace, he leaped to his feet, grabbing the rope at the same time. He gave it a hard pull. It slackened enough for him to reach for the knot and release himself from the loop.

"¡Eh! hombre negro," he heard behind him.

In one swift movement, Bose whirled around into a crouch and drew his gun at the same time. He clicked the chamber over to put a shell in front of the firing pin. His eyes focused on a Mexican caballero sitting on a horse, brandishing a rifle at him. The man was less than fifteen yards away, but that was not a very close target for his weapon.

"I would not do that, Señor," said another man, again behind him.

Bose stiffened as he heard the distinct sound of a pistol being cocked. Without waiting another second, he jumped to his left and rolled. There was a shot. He came to a stop ready to fire at the man who had offered the warning, but he held back his thumb from the hammer when he saw Jake holding one arm around the vaquero's throat while he held his gun to the man's temple.

"You dumb nigger," said Jake, "y'all are constantly into some kinda trouble. If it don't come your way, you have to go lookin' for it."

"I could've handled them, Jake," said Bose as he stood up, dusting himself.

"Sure, y'all could," humored Jake. "This here greaser was about to put a bullet into that black hide of yours, and you say you could handle it." The other Mexican made a move with his rifle. Jake pulled the hammer back on his gun. "No, no, no, compadre. Y'all just drop that thing or your friend here will never eat another tortilla." He choked the man he held to emphasize his point.

The white man Bose had seen earlier came riding onto the scene with a half dozen more Mexicans behind him.

"What in the hell is goin' on here?" he demanded after halting his horse a few paces away from Bose.

"Easy does it, mister," said Bose as he raised his gun in the man's direction.

"Y'all ramroddin' this bunch of greasers?" asked Jake.

"The name is Campbell," said the man. "These boys work for me, and I work for Jim Burleson."

Campbell was a grizzled old man who had seen many a day on the ranges of Texas, as witnessed by his leathery

skin. He wasn't about to start any trouble but was ready
to finish it if any came his way.

"I've heard tell of that name before," said Jake. "I also
heard the name Campbell. Y'all wouldn't be the same
Campbell who rode with Sam Tatum, would you?"

"Three years Sam and me was together," said Campbell. He squinted at Jake. "Yep. Even from here I can see
that you favor him. You wouldn't be his boy, would you?"

"Just his pride and joy," said Jake as he lowered his revolver.

"Well, I knowed Sam Tatum to be a good man, and I
s'pect his son would have to be the same."

"Well, thank you kindly, Mr. Campbell. Pappy said the
same of you every time he spoke of the times y'all spent
together."

"What'd your pappy name you, son?"

"He wanted to name me after you, but Mom wouldn't
have me called Aloysius for the world. She wanted Hez-
ekiah, but they compromised and give me the name of
Jacob. 'Most everyone calls me Jake."

"Well, then, Jake, what seems to be the trouble here?"

"These two greasers was givin' my friend here a bad
time," explained Jake as he motioned toward Bose. "I
sorta stepped in and stopped it."

"I see," said Campbell. "Well, I'll handle them now."

Jake released his prisoner. "Get back to the herd, Ra-
mírez." Campbell turned in his saddle. "That goes for all
you lazy buzzards. Now get back to work."

The vaqueros departed, leaving Campbell to visit with
Jake and Bose. Burleson's trail boss told them he had
owned the herd he was driving to the Bosque before
selling it to Burleson. Part of the deal was for the old man
to take the cattle to New Mexico. It wasn't until after
they had consummated the deal that Burleson told him
that most of the hands were going to be Mexicans.

"I don't like greasers and never have," said Campbell.
"If I'd known about this bunch before signin' the papers,
I'd never have sold. Now I'm stuck with them."

"What y'all need is someone to make them work," said
Jake. "If I wasn't already holdin' a job, I'd be glad to do
it."

"This man you're workin' for," said Campbell, "I've
heard of him. Yankee lover, I hear. Is he as straight a man
as they say?"

"Mr. Lovin' is the most honest man in Texas," said
Bose.

"That's right," concurred Jake. "Him and Mr. Goodnight is as straight as they come. A man knows he's gettin'
a fair shake from both of them. It was a real lucky day
when I went to work for Mr. Lovin'."

"I wish I had a few of you boys with me," said Campbell. "It'd sure make this drive a lot easier. Really
could've used you when them Apaches jumped us the
other day."

Jake gave Bose a sideways glance. "How was that, Mr.
Campbell?"

"It was about thirty miles back, almost a week ago," he
began. "A whole bunch of them red devils come ridin'
down on us. Those greasers ran off like scared rabbits as
soon as they saw them comin'. The Apaches cut out a few
head and run off with our pack mules and extra horses.
They hardly fired a shot, it was so easy for them. Damned
greasers never raised a gun at them. Me and Whitey got
off a few shots, but we didn't hit anything but air."

"We'd best tell Mr. Goodnight about this," said Bose.
"He's already worried about Mr. Lovin'."

"Yeah, we'd best do that," agreed Jake. "Well, Mr.
Campbell, it was right nice meetin' you after all my
pappy told me about y'all."

The two white men shook hands and said their fare-

wells. Campbell gave Bose a nod, and the black cowboy
returned the gesture. The old man's bigotry wasn't limited to Mexicans.

Bose and Jake reported the incident and Campbell's
story to Goodnight. The cowman's concern for his partner
was increased after the telling of the tale. He immediately
ordered the men to quicken the pace of the herd.

Early the next morning, the outfit overtook Campbell
and his Mexicans. After a brief conference between
Goodnight and the old man, they agreed to combine their
efforts and resources. Goodnight felt sorry for the former
Ranger, because he was stuck with the Mexicans and because they were without provisions since the Apache raid.
He promised Campbell that his men would see to it that
the caballeros did an honest day's work for a change.

Two days later they came to a bend in the Pecos where
a mountain jutted out from its range to the edge of the
river. From the valley below, a cave could be seen halfway up its side. Goodnight noted it as a good place for
Indians to hide for an ambush. He ordered Bose and Jake
to ride with him to scout the position.

At a curve in the trail, Bose noticed something emerge
from the opening. A man, he thought. He wasn't sure.
Goodnight saw him too. The man beckoned to them, but
Goodnight held back, suspecting an Indian trick to lure
them to their deaths. The man motioned toward them
again. Goodnight straightened in his saddle to take a better look.

"It's Billy, Mr. Goodnight," said Bose as he recognized
the man in the cave.

"By God, it is Billy!" exclaimed Goodnight. He whipped
his horse with the quirt to gallop up the hill. Bose and
Jake followed single file.

"Good Lord, man," said Goodnight as he jumped down

from his mount in front of his friend, "what happened to you?"

Wilson couldn't speak at first. Tears cut a course down his emaciated cheeks through the dried, red dirt that seemed to cover every inch of his body. His clothes, what was left of them, were caked with the soil. His feet were bare and bleeding. His face was hollow but filled with the joy of being saved from death.

Bose took a canteen from his saddle and uncorked it. He handed it to Goodnight to offer a drink to Wilson, who refused with a shake of his head. He collapsed in Goodnight's arms.

"Help me get him into the shade," said Goodnight.

Bose and Jake each grabbed a leg as Goodnight held him under his armpits. They carried Wilson back to the mouth of the cave, where they laid him on the ground. Goodnight offered the water again, and Billy accepted it.

"Injuns jumped us three days out," he said after a hard swallow on the canteen. "Apaches. They came out of nowhere. Shot Mr. Lovin' in the arm and side. He sent me to get help." His voice cracked. "Don't know if he's still alive."

Goodnight was swift to act. He sent Jake back to get help for Wilson. Bose was ordered to find Campbell and bring him on the run. Within minutes, both were back at the cave.

"Mister Campbell, can you get one of your men to go with me to find Mr. Loving?" asked Goodnight.

"I'll go with you myself," said Campbell.

"I thought you would," said Goodnight.

"I'm goin' too," said Jake.

"So am I," said Bose. "I should've gone with Mr. Lovin' in the first place." Goodnight gave him a hard look. "You can't stop me, Mr. Goodnight. I said I was goin'." He eyed Jake, who nodded once in return. "We're both goin'."

"It doesn't look like I'm going to change your mind," said Goodnight. "All right, you go. Mr. Campbell, since we seem to be making an expedition out of this, you might as well bring another man along. That will make five of us. Jake, you get some provisions from the chuck wagon. Bose, you pass the word to the men about what we're up to."

Bose rode off to tell the other drovers about Goodnight's decision, while Jake met Otis Kinney, who was bringing the chuck wagon to the scene as fast as he could.

In the meantime, Billy Wilson told Goodnight everything he could recall about the past few days.

Wilson and Loving were traveling as Goodnight prescribed, riding at night and hiding by day. After two days and three nights, Loving decided, since they hadn't seen any sign of Indians, that it was safe to ride during the day.

Late in the afternoon of the third day, an Apache war party rode down on them from the hills next to the river. The white men ran for cover, finding a defendable post behind a sand dune with the river to protect their backs. They pulled their horses to the ground and opened up a steady fire on the red raiders.

Wilson estimated the hostiles to be around a dozen in number. They fanned out in a half circle. The Indians had only a few guns, but they were enough. In the first few minutes of the fight, Loving was hit twice; once in the left wrist and a clean shot through his right side above the hip. The bullet that struck his arm shattered the bone, making his hand almost useless.

They managed to keep the Indians at bay until darkness settled on them. Loving was certain he was a dead man, so he couldn't see any reason for Billy to die with him. He ordered Wilson to go for help, but the cowboy argued the point. Loving was adamant. As his companion slipped down to the river, the cowman sent the horses in the opposite direction to distract the Apaches.

Wilson swam the river, crossing to the other side. All that night he followed its course south, sometimes walking, sometimes swimming. The next day he decided to hide and rest. Toward late afternoon he renewed his trek to find Goodnight and the herd. He continued as he had the night before; by land when possible, by water when necessary. During the second morning, he discovered the cave, where he collapsed from exhaustion. The bawling of the cattle awakened him just before Goodnight found him.

Goodnight felt there might be a chance that Loving was still alive. The odds of it were slim, but he was willing to risk everything to save his partner.

Campbell selected the same Mexican who had jumped Bose as the fifth man in the search for Loving. The old man was suspicious of this caballero, because he was rumored to have once ridden with the Comancheros, those bandidos who trafficked in stolen cattle and kidnaped children. It was the man's knowledge of Indians that prompted Campbell to choose him.

The next morning, the five rescuers came upon the place Wilson had described to Goodnight as the scene of the fight. Loving, dead or alive, should be there. They halted at the base of a hill, which Goodnight and Campbell climbed on foot in order to survey the sight.

"What do you think, Mr. Campbell?" the younger man asked as they looked down on the quiet valley below them. There was no sign of Indians, but that didn't mean they weren't there.

"He could be down there," admitted Campbell, "and there could be a dozen red devils all around him hidin' in the bushes. I think we oughta ride down there lickety-split with our guns lettin' anyone there know we're comin'."

"It's a bold move," said Goodnight, "but I think it is a time for bravado."

He moved to return to the others, who were with the horses, but Campbell stopped him.

"One thing, Goodnight. That Mex may have thoughts of joinin' up with those Injuns. If he makes a move to leave us, I'll see that it's his last. I'd rather I did it, because he's my responsibility."

Goodnight gave a knowing nod, and they went back to the others. He informed his men of what they had decided. Each man mounted up, filled a hand with a weapon, checked it to make certain it had a bullet ready, then gave Goodnight a sign he was ready. The cowman nodded and kicked his horse into a full gallop as he led the party over the hill.

They topped the crest and rode down the slope at full speed, yelling at the tops of their voices but not firing until fired upon. Across the flat they raced toward the dune Goodnight felt was the one Loving and Wilson had defended. The only sounds they heard were their own as they dashed to the sand knoll and over it. There was no shooting, no more yelling, no Indian war cries, and no Loving. They drew up on their mounts. They were simultaneously disappointed and relieved.

"This is where it was, all right," said Goodnight. "See there? Blood on the sand. Empty cartridges, broken arrows. The Indians must've got him." He wiped his forearm over his eyes. "Let's spread out and see if we can find what's left of him."

They moved about the surrounding area, looking for the body they didn't really want to find.

"Mr. Goodnight, over here!" shouted Bose from the edge of the river.

The other four men joined him.

"Find something, Bose?" asked Goodnight cautiously.

"Take a look," he said as he pointed to a piece of bloody cloth hanging limp from a bush on the bank. "Looks to me like it come from Mr. Lovin's shirt."

"It does at that," agreed Goodnight as he reached down to retrieve the rag. He inspected it closer. "Yes, I have to say this came from his shirt. He must have slipped away from them, taking to the river as Billy did. There's no telling where he is now, but one thing's for certain. He has to be dead."

That wasn't what he wanted to admit, but he knew he had to face that fact sooner or later. Without further words, he turned his horse to start back down the river. The others quietly followed. Late that night they rejoined the herd.

The news about Loving was kept from Billy Wilson until he was strong enough to take it. Goodnight, Bose, and Jake avoided seeing him until Otis Kinney said Wilson was definitely on the mend. On their third day back, the cook sent word to Goodnight that Billy would recover from his ordeal in the desert.

Goodnight was out scouting when Frank Willborn caught up with him to give him Kinney's message. He sent Willborn back to his duties, but he delayed going to the chuck wagon to speak to Wilson as he searched his soul for the courage to face his friend.

As he procrastinated, Jim Burleson came over a hill ahead of him. Burleson had become apprehensive about his overdue herd and had ridden out to find it. Goodnight immediately informed him when they met that his cattle were in good hands.

"That makes me glad," said Burleson, relieved by the

news. He was near the same age as Goodnight but looked younger, because he hadn't spent as much time on the range as Goodnight. He removed his hat and wiped his forehead with his shirt sleeve. He replaced the Stetson and squinted at Goodnight as they sat atop their horses. "By the way, your partner wants to see you as soon as you can ride to Sumner."

"Loving is dead!" snapped Goodnight.

Burleson was taken aback. "I tell you, he's alive and at Fort Sumner. He's been shot up, but he is alive. I helped bring him in."

Goodnight looked hard into the eyes of the man. He decided he was hearing the truth.

"This is great news, Burleson!" exclaimed the cowman.

"He's very anxious to see you, Goodnight. I don't know what the urgency is. His wounds are minor, and he did seem to be recovering."

"I will leave immediately," said Goodnight. "I'm as anxious to see him as he is to see me."

The cowman went back to the herd to tell everyone of Burleson's report. The first man he reached was Bose.

"Loving is alive and in Sumner!" shouted the ecstatic Goodnight as he rode up.

Bose drew up his horse. "Alive?"

"Yes, alive," reiterated Goodnight, grinning his pleasure at the telling. He motioned over his shoulder toward Burleson, who was following at a slower pace. "That's Jim Burleson. He has just now come from Loving."

Bose ripped off his hat and gave it a spinning toss into the air. With a joyous yell, he kicked his mount and sped after the sombrero, catching it before it could touch the earth. He continued to the chuck wagon, yahooing like a man gone loco all the way.

Otis Kinney saw him coming, his hat waving wildly over his head. Then he heard him. Kinney felt a stir of excitement as he halted the mules. Billy Wilson heard the clamor and poked his head out of the wagon next to Kinney.

"What's all the fuss, Otis?" asked Wilson.

"It's Bose," said Kinney. "I think that boy's been in the sun too long."

The black cowboy rode up to the wagon at a full gallop, then jerked his mount to a dead stop next to it. In the same motion, he leaped from the saddle onto the seat next to the cook. He grabbed Wilson by the arms and shook him, almost violently.

"He's alive, Billy!" shouted the exuberant youth right in Wilson's face. "He's alive!"

Wilson put his hands on Bose's shoulders to calm him. "Who's alive, boy?"

"Mr. Lovin', that's who. He's alive and in Fort Sumner."

"Glory be," said Kinney softly.

Wilson was incredulous as he began shaking Bose, too. "Alive? Lovin's alive?"

Although no one had told him Loving might be dead, the cowboy with the shriveled arm had already assumed it.

"Yessir, he's alive!" exclaimed Bose again.

"Praise the Lord!" shouted Billy. "Praise the Lord!" He pulled Bose against him, hugging and slapping him on the back. Tears welled up and fell happily from his eyes. "Praise the Lord," he cried softly.

A ripple of good cheer followed Goodnight around the herd as he went from man to man in their outfit spreading the glad tidings. Shouts not unlike those Bose had just finished were heard from every corner as each man expressed his delight at the very good news.

Within the hour, Goodnight was mounted on the best mule in the remuda and on his way to join Loving at Fort

Sumner. It was all he could do to stop the rest of the men from going with him.

Goodnight had his reunion with Loving at the military post, then went about some business that the older man sent him on to Santa Fe. On his return from the capital, a messenger met him on the trail to tell him Loving had taken a turn for the worse. The wound in his partner's side had healed, but the injury to his wrist had not responded as hoped. Gangrene had set into it. Goodnight rushed back to the army fort to be with his friend.

The trail herd under the direction of Billy Wilson had reached the Bosque by this time. The hands were eager to take time off to visit Loving in the post hospital, but Wilson wouldn't let anyone go, because Goodnight had left explicit orders that they were to stay with the herd until his return.

The doctor at the fort was reluctant to amputate Loving's arm to stop the disease. Loving was also against the idea, because he didn't trust the young physician, who had only recently come to America from Scotland. Goodnight didn't care what either of them thought. He demanded that the arm come off immediately, because he knew his partner wouldn't live very long if the infection spread out of his arm.

The operation was performed, and at the first it was thought to be a success. Then the main artery ruptured, and Loving had to undergo the knife again. In spite of his amazing constitution, which had sustained him through his ordeal in the desert and the first operation, he was unable to rally a third time. He lived twenty-two days, lucid to the last.

Realizing he was drawing close to the end of his life, Loving requested a visit from each of the men who had worked for him on his final drive. Each came, stayed a few minutes, then departed saddened by what they knew would be a great loss. The last man to see him was Bose.

Loving was propped up in bed with pillows when Bose entered the sickroom, which wasn't much bigger than a cell. The patient's resting place was pushed against the wall beneath the one small, dirty window, which was kept closed. A nightstand with a pitcher of water and a glass stood next to the bed, and a simple wooden chair was at its foot.

"Sit down, Bose," said Loving, his voice a pitch higher and much weaker than the black cowboy recalled. The dying man motioned with his remaining hand toward the chair. The hand, once strong and firm, was withered and quivering.

Bose moved as directed, fumbling with the back of the chair and awkwardly sitting down on it. The shock of seeing his employer in his deathbed was struck across the youth's face. Tears already had him glassy-eyed. His lower lip quivered on occasion.

"Bose, I wanted to see you last because I have a special request of you. Your being a Negro, life doesn't offer too many opportunities for you. I admit I once had my doubts about you, but they were all predicated on the color of your skin. After these past two years, I know now that I was very wrong. I couldn't have asked more from any man than what you gave me in performing your duties. I want to thank you for that.

"I also want to give you some advice, Bose. I have become very fond of you these past two years, and I would like to die knowing that you are going to become more than a drover who will grow old and die before your time. I know you can handle yourself in a fight now, but that might not always be so. There may come a time when you will run up against someone who is a little better with a gun. Of course, you know I don't really abide by guns, but I accept them as a necessary evil in this land until the day comes when men can settle their differences peace-fully and according to the law.

"That brings up the precise point of this conversation. Because you are black-skinned, the law looks upon you in a different way. It's a white man's law, but that doesn't make it just. This is a white man's world, and black people have to accept that for now. There may come a time when every man will be accepted for what he can do and not for the color of his skin. But I don't believe that day is close at hand.

"Because you are a Negro, your choices in life are limited, but you do have some. I know your folks have a farm near Weatherford. Your father was wise to get that farm. One day it will be yours, and when it is, use it wisely. Take up farming if you have to, but raise cattle, too. You know how. Build yourself a good ranch and farm. You can do it. You have to if you ever want to be anything. Get yourself a good woman who will stand by you no matter what tragedy may strike. Have some children and see that they get some book learning.

"Bose, you stand on the threshold of a new day, and it is up to you to see that new day gets a good start. If you can't make a place for yourself in this world, you can at least make a place for your children and your grandchildren and every child born after that. But it all has to start with you.

"Now to another matter. I've made Mr. Goodnight promise to keep our partnership for another two years until the debts are settled. I want you to stick with him until that time when the partnership is finally dissolved. He and I have already discussed this matter to some length, and we are agreed that it is for the best. When he has finished our agreement, he will help you get settled into farming with your folks.

"What I want from you, Bose, is your promise that you will heed my advice and get out of this end of the business and into an endeavor of your own. Will you give me your promise?"

The anguish in the young man's heart rose to his throat, encumbering his ability to speak. The dam that held back the water in his eyes finally burst. He buried his face in his hands and wept.

"Now, don't carry on so," comforted Loving. "People die every day. That's a fact everyone must face sooner or later. A man's life is only remembered by how he affected the people he came in contact with. Realizing that is why I am asking this of you. If I can die knowing you will amount to more than a saddle tramp, I will pass away a happy man. Now, can I have your promise?"

Bose wiped his eyes, temporarily drying them. "Yessir, Mr. Lovin', I promise to do exactly as you say. I'll become somethin' and make a good life for myself and for my children. I promise, Mr. Lovin'."

Then he broke down again.

"Thank you, son. I can go in peace now."

Bose looked up through a watery blur. Loving's eyes were closed and his breathing was almost too shallow to be seen or heard. Bose was sure his employer was dead. He leaped from his chair and ran from the room. Without saying a word to the men waiting outside, he kept on going straight to his horse, leaping on its back and riding away from the fort as fast as the animal carrying him would run.

He let the mare have her head as she raced down the road to Santa Fe until she became winded. Bose let her walk a few miles before dismounting and walking with her. The pain subsided, and he began to think again. By the time night fell, he was determined to live up to his promise to the fullest of his ability and at all costs.

TEN

With Oliver Loving gone, Goodnight continued the partnership with James Loving, the eldest son. The new partners knew each other already, and neither particularly cared for the other. James considered Goodnight to be an ignorant cowboy, while the cowman thought of the younger Loving as an overeducated buffoon. Now they were thrust together, and each decided to put personal opinions aside in favor of business.

For his part, Bose knew James Loving to be unlike his father. Whereas the parent was tolerant and benevolent, the son was bigoted and arrogant. These were faults the black cowboy couldn't cope with. Although he was legally in the employ of Loving by virtue of the trail agreement he had signed before leaving Texas, Bose decided to switch his allegiance to Goodnight, a man he respected and who returned that respect.

The first order of business for Goodnight was to establish a new ranch in Colorado. He chose to leave the spread on the Bosque to Loving for the younger man to do with as he pleased. The new place, on Apishapa Creek, in southeastern Colorado, would belong exclusively to Goodnight. The separation of lands didn't mean a division of the cattle. On the contrary, the cattle would remain under joint ownership.

Due to the partnership, Goodnight was forced to spend much of his time away from the Colorado ranch. He placed Billy Wilson in charge, with Bose to ramrod the men on the range. This suited both men fine. Wilson supervised the construction of buildings and corrals, while Bose saw to it that the cattle were tended properly.

Everything went peacefully for the first few months, until a man named Fisher rode onto the spread one day late in the summer of 1868. The man wasn't very impressive to look at. Patches of whiskers in varying colors and lengths covered his cheeks and chin but failed to hide the trail dust that was accumulated on his skin. The tattered clothing he wore was just as filthy, and he smelled like four skunks that had been dead for a week. The roan horse he rode was a good match for him. It was all skin and bones and shaggy hair. The trappings on it had also seen better days. When he dismounted and approached Billy Wilson, the foreman quickly caught a whiff of the odor emanating from the visitor and moved upwind.

"What's your business, stranger?" asked Billy, already suspicious of the man.

"The name is Fisher," he said through tobacco-stained teeth. "I seen some cows what belong to me out on the prairie near here. Just wanted you to know I was gonna cut them out and take them back to my place over by Trinidad."

"Is that so?" Wilson was definitely wary of this man Fisher. "Well, you just go ahead, but be sure you only take those that have your brand."

Fisher nodded and climbed back on his mount. The poor animal seemed to groan when the man situated himself in the saddle. He rode off toward the east.

"Who was that?" asked Bose as he came out of the house.

"Said his name's Fisher," answered Billy absently. He studied the disappearing rider. "That might be it, but I don't think he was tellin' the truth about his business here. A man that ragged sure don't own a ranch of his own. You best follow him, Bose, and see that he don't take none of Mr. Goodnight's stock."

"Take Mr. Goodnight's stock?" quizzed Bose.

"That's right. He claimed to have seen some of his own cows mixed in with ours. I kind of doubt that. You best see that he don't take none that don't rightfully belong to him."

Bose understood. He mounted his horse and rode off in pursuit of the stranger. By the time he caught up with Fisher, the man was already cutting out a few head.

"Say, what do you think you're doin' there?" demanded Ikard when he came onto the scene.

"What's it to you, nigger?" snapped Fisher.

Bose saved his breath and threw down on the white man. His thumb pulled back on the hammer of the Colt and cut loose a round between the legs of Fisher's horse. The roan reared when the bullet ricocheted off a rock, throwing stone chips and sparks against the animal's fetlocks. Fisher had all he could handle trying to settle the mare.

"What the hell'd you do that for, nigger?"

Bose cocked the gun again and shot off Fisher's hat.

"Damn it, man, what's come over you?" screamed the frightened man.

"No one calls me nigger," said Bose as he readied the pistol for a third shot.

"I'm sorry, friend," pleaded Fisher, who wasn't heeled. "I didn't mean nothin' by it."

Bose took careful aim.

"You gotta believe me. I'm real sorry." Fisher's face paled, even through the dirt on it, with a certainty that he was about to meet his Maker. "For God's sake, don't kill me. I got a wife and young uns. They need me. Please don't kill me."

Bose doubted he was old enough to have a wife, and

the man's appearance didn't add credence to the story. He relaxed his thumb from the hammer. "Now back to my first question," said the black cowboy. "What do you think you're doin' with Mr. Lovin's and Mr. Goodnight's cows?"

"These are my cows," insisted Fisher, suddenly ready to make an argument.

"They don't have any brand on them but the one I put there myself," said Bose. "I know these cows. They belong to Mr. Lovin' and Mr. Goodnight, and no one else got one single right to them unless they got papers what say they done bought them. You got that, white trash?"

"I tell you—" Fisher began, but the click of the Colt being cocked again finished the sentence for him.

"Tell me what?" asked Bose casually.

"I guess I'll be movin' along," said Fisher. He turned his horse and drifted away under Bose's watchful eye.

Early the next morning, Fisher returned to the Apishapa ranch, only this time he wasn't alone. Riding with him were eleven armed Mexicans, who looked more like Comancheros than vaqueros.

The crew at the ranch were just finishing breakfast when Fisher and his bunch appeared outside the bunkhouse door. Besides Wilson and Ikard, Jake Tatum, Frank Willborn, Billy Taylor, "Long" Joe Loving, and Otis Kinney were lighting up their rolled cigarets for an after-meal smoke. They leaned back in their chairs, relaxing before going to work.

"Hey, there in the bunkhouse!" they heard Fisher call out to them. Bose was closest to a window. He peered out to see the would-be tough and his cohort.

"That saddle tramp is back," he said casually to Billy Wilson. "He's got a bunch of Mexicans with him this time."

Wilson rose from his chair. "Guess I'd best see what he

wants." He opened the door, closed it behind him as he stepped onto the porch. Unheeled, he stepped to the edge of the plank veranda, his arms folded in front of him. "I thought you were told once that this is Mr. Goodnight's spread and those are his cattle out there on the range."

Fisher leaned forward on his horse's neck. "Well, I don't see no Mr. Goodnight here to tell me those ain't my cattle out there. All I see is a cripple-arm old goat tellin' me somethin' I don't want to hear. These boys here don't want to hear you talk no more neither. They just want to get my cows and get out of here."

Billy eyed the Mexicans. They were a sorry lot. Every one of them needed a bath and a shave, and a new set of duds would have helped too. What they didn't need was more weapons. Each caballero carried two pistols on his hips, and a rifle stuck out of a saddle scabbard on every horse. The Mexicans were spread out in a line to each side of Fisher. Wilson didn't have to look at each one to know they were waiting for him to make a move that might be his last.

"You were told yesterday," said Wilson, "you ain't got no cows around here. Now, get yourself away from here."

"Well, compadres," Fisher began, but the sound of several hammers being locked into firing position cut him short.

"You heard the man," said Bose as he stepped out onto the porch, the Colt in his left hand and the Henry rifle in his right.

One Mexican to the far left of Fisher went for his guns, but Bose dropped him before he could clear leather. A second vaquero made his move, but a bullet from a bunkhouse window ripped the man's sombrero from his head. The horses danced about as their riders fought to control them. The man Bose had shot was on the ground holding his wounded chest and writhing in pain. One Mexican turned tail and ran off.

"You best follow him," said Wilson, still standing straight and calm. "If you don't, you'll wind up like him."

Wilson didn't have to point at whom he meant. Fisher and the others knew he was referring to the dying man.

"You ain't heard the last of me," said Fisher in a parting shot. He motioned a hand at the dead caballero. Two others jumped down from their horses, picked up the body, and draped it over the deceased's saddle. *"Vámanos, muchachos."* At Fisher's command, the band of would-be rustlers were off.

"For a minute there," confessed Wilson as he watched them ride away, "I thought we was gonna have dead greasers all over the place. That would've been a fine mess to clean up."

"I don't think Mr. Goodnight would've liked that too much," said Bose. "You know how he feels about Mexicans."

"Yeah, it would've made him real unhappy," said Billy. "There ain't no use in us upsettin' the man. He's got enough problems already."

The episode with Fisher had yet to reach its climax.

Goodnight returned to the ranch with another herd from Texas, brought north by James Loving as far as the Bosque and the rest of the way by Goodnight. Loving remained in New Mexico to fulfill the contracts the partnership still had with the military.

No one told the cowman about Fisher and his Mexicans, but Goodnight didn't have to hear about the incident from his own men. News of the confrontation spread throughout southeastern Colorado, once Fisher began to brag about how he was going to get even with the Texas outfit.

Fisher was not a man to fear, but he had a friend who

was. Bill Coe was his name, and he was given a wide berth by all who knew him by sight or by reputation. Because law and order were still rare commodities in that part of the country, Coe and his gang had an easy time of it as they preyed on small settlements, ranchers, and freight haulers. He didn't like Texans coming into his territory, because he knew they would bring civilized ways with them. Goodnight's growing prestige as a decent and honest man scared Coe more than a hangman's noose.

Goodnight was resting quietly when a messenger came from the mayor of Trinidad, a small community a day's ride from the Apishapa ranch. Bose brought the terrified little Mexican into Goodnight's presence in the main house. Although roused from a needed sleep period, the rancher was amicable with the visitor.

"Mr. Goodnight, this man says he comes from Trinidad," said Bose as he held the Mexican at gunpoint. "He said somethin' about Bill Coe and his gang holdin' the town."

"Is that so?" queried Goodnight as he slipped into his boots.

"*Si, señor,*" said the messenger anxiously. "*El señor alcalde* say for you to come *muy pronto.*"

"The mayor sent you?" quizzed Goodnight.

The Mexican nodded.

"*¿Cómo se llama el alcalde?*"

"*El alcalde se llama Ortega,*" answered the man.

"Well, at least he knows the mayor's name," said Goodnight.

"*Por favor, señor,*" the messenger pleaded, "things are not good in Trinidad. *El señor alcalde* wants you to come quick."

"I believe this man really is from the mayor of Trinidad. I think we should call on the gentleman and offer our services. Bose, get a dozen men ready to ride and have them armed for a real good fight. I don't think Coe will stand up to us, but you can never tell what a rattlesnake like him is going to do."

Within the hour, the Texans were raising a dust cloud as they rode hard to Trinidad.

The messenger led them straight to the mayor's home, on the north side of the town. Ortega, a slight man with trim mustaches on each side of his upper lip, greeted them at the front gate of his adobe hacienda. His face was colorless, with bulging eyes that bespoke the anxiety that burned inside him.

Goodnight had met the man previously. He found Ortega to be a very hospitable ranchero in the old tradition of Spain. The quiet yet gracious demeanor of the official had set well with the tall Texan. He liked the man right from the onset of their relationship.

"Señor Goodnight," Ortega began as he nervously shook the cowman's hand, "I am so glad to see you. Thank you so much for coming. I cannot begin to tell you of the terrible things that are happening in my town."

"I have enough imagination to spare you that distasteful task, *señor alcalde*," replied Goodnight as he clasped the mayor's hand with a firm grip. "I have brought some men to rid your people of this pestilence."

Ortega looked past Goodnight at the armed cowboys. Each man possessed a keen determination to meet the challenge ahead of them. Their rugged dispositions served to ease the fears in the mayor's heart.

"I am so grateful, Señor Goodnight," said Ortega, "but I do not wish there to be any bloodshed if it can be avoided."

"Neither do I, *señor alcalde*. I would like to settle this matter as peaceably as we can, but if there has to be a fight, then we will fight."

"Yes," said Ortega reluctantly, "what must be done,

must be done." He hesitated to say anything further but
then found the courage to speak the words he knew he
had to say. "I will get my gun and come with you."

"That won't be necessary," said Goodnight. "You just
leave this business to us. There is no need to involve yourself or any of your people. My men and I will handle Coe
and his bunch."

The mayor, relieved by the refusal, watched Goodnight
remount his horse and lead his men toward the main
street of Trinidad. Ortega crossed himself and said a silent prayer for the safety of his benefactor and the cowboys who rode with him.

Trinidad was a very old village, dating back to the days
when Spain ruled the lands north of the Rio Grande. The
main street had all of the businesses on one side or the
other of it, and there were a few other streets intersecting
and paralleling it. Some of the buildings along the avenue
were wooden structures, but most were adobe or brick.
All of them faced the dusty thoroughfare. Only two were
more than one story: the bank and the hotel.

Goodnight deployed his men in a straight line, six to
each side of him, as they walked their horses slowly into
the town. It was late evening, a slight glow of pink still
caressing the peaks to the west. The stars were already
twinkling, and the moon was full over the eastern horizon. The only sounds to disturb the peaceful setting came
from the south end of town, a long two hundred yards
away from the Texans. The revelry from the two saloons
dissipated as they moved closer, until at last only the
squeaking of leather on leather and the soft, plodding
steps of their horses could be heard.

"Hold up, boys," said Goodnight. "Let's give them a
moment to decide what they're going to do."

The Texans waited. A grim resolve passively shaped
their features.

"Let's have it out with them sonsabitches!" they heard a man shout from behind the saloon.

"I said ride!" came another man's angry voice from the same vicinity.

There followed the pounding hoofbeats of horses fading into the night.

"It could be a trap," said Billy Wilson.

"Could be," said Goodnight. "Bose, you take three men and ride down behind those buildings." Goodnight indicated the structures to his right. "Billy, you take three men and go down the other side. The rest of you go real slow with me."

Bose led Jake, Frank, and Billy Taylor down a side street, then south down another street behind the buildings. They moved deliberately, with caution dictating every step. At the end of the street was a barn and corral. Two horses, saddled and ready to ride, were tied to the fence rail. Bose motioned for Jake and Frank to go around to the back of the stable while he and Taylor approached the front.

"Come back here, you!" they heard a familiar voice shout inside the barn.

The door burst open, and a Mexican girl came running out. Bose and Taylor threw down on her but held their fire. The girl screamed at the sight of the two blacks aiming their pistols at her. Bose waved her away with the barrel of his Colt, and the girl ran into the back of the saloon.

"We know you're in there," said Bose, a steady rhythm in his voice. "Toss out your gun and come out with your hands high over your head."

"I'm comin' out," said the man after a moment's delay. A revolver preceded his exit from the barn. "Don't shoot me. I ain't heeled."

"Well, now, if it ain't Mr. Fisher, the cattle baron,"

mocked Bose when he recognized the desperado. "What are you doin' here, white trash?"

"Just havin' a little fun," said Fisher. "That's all."

"You're comin' up in the world, ain't you, Fisher? What with you ridin' with Bill Coe, you're becomin' a regular bad man. You keep that up and they're gonna have your name posted all over. They might even put a bounty on your no-account head."

Bose put his gun away, and Taylor did the same as both of them dismounted. Fisher took advantage of the opportunity to make a play for his gun. Bose, hoping Fisher would do something stupid, kicked the pistol out of his reach, drawing his own at the same time. He grabbed Fisher by his shirt front and shoved the barrel of his revolver in the man's face. He spun Fisher as he lifted him from the ground. Bose wound up with his back to the barn door. Billy moved in beside him, also back to the opening.

"I should've just shot you dead," growled Bose, "but that ain't the way Mr. Goodnight wants it. He says we got to be as peaceable as we can."

He pushed Fisher away from him. Billy stooped to retrieve the gun. Jake and Frank came around the barn and joined them.

"I see y'all caught yourself a skunk," said Jake.

"Just one," said Bose. "See anything back there?"

"Nope. Looks like he was all that was left."

"What happened to the others?" Bose asked Fisher.

"They musta run off," he replied. "I heard them come out of the saloon, but they rode off before I could get my pants on."

"That's too bad," said Bose. He looked at the two horses tied to the fence. "Who them hosses belong to?"

"One's mine," said Fisher. "I don't know who the other one belongs to."

"He's lyin'," said Jake. "I got a rope that'll stretch the truth out of him."

"Don't bother none," said Bose. "There ain't no sense in breakin' his scrawny neck. We'll let Mr. Goodnight decide what to do with him."

Fisher's eyes glared past Bose for a second before he leaped against the black cowboy, knocking him to the ground. A gun fired, the shot coming from the open barn door. Bose rolled to the ground, separating Fisher from him. He came to a kneeling position just as a second shot flashed out of the darkness. Bose fanned the hammer of his Colt in the direction of the flare of light, emptying the cylinder of its five cartridges. There was no return fire, only a man's scream. Quiet settled on the stable area.

Billy Taylor, Jake, and Frank had their guns ready for further action, but none was forthcoming. Seconds later, with the shooting stopped, a death rattle came from within the barn.

"Sounds like y'all got him," said Jake.

Fisher was sprawled on the ground next to Bose. He lifted his head, sadness drooping his face.

"Good-bye, Hec," he said softly.

"You know that man?" asked Bose. He rose to his full height.

"We growed up together," said Fisher quietly.

"How come you didn't let him kill me?" asked Bose. "How come you saved my life instead of his?"

Fisher cleared his throat before answering. "I didn't think you was gonna kill him. I thought if I saved you, it would go easier on me and Hec. I didn't think you was gonna kill him."

Bose offered a hand to Fisher to help him up. The white man accepted the assist. Their hands stayed clasped together for an extra heartbeat. Their eyes met.

"Thanks for savin' my life," said Bose. Then he said, "I'm sorry about your friend."

"Hec was my brother," said Fisher, his head hung low.

Goodnight and the rest of the outfit rode up with their guns at the ready.

"We heard shooting," said Goodnight. He looked at all the men, surveying each, making certain all were accounted for. "What happened here?"

"You tell him, Jake," said Bose as he put his Colt away and walked toward his horse.

Jake kept his words brief as he explained the incident. Goodnight listened carefully. He nodded when Jake finished, mulling over what he should do with Fisher.

"Well, friend," said Goodnight, "you seem to be traveling in bad company. I think a bath, a shave, and a new set of clothes might make a decent man of you. Some honest work is definitely in order too. Bose, I want you to see that he gets all those things. Is that agreeable to you, Mr. Fisher?"

"Yessir, Mr. Goodnight, sir," said Fisher, surprised at Goodnight's generosity. He had actually expected the Texans to hang him.

"Get on your hoss, Fisher," said Bose. "We gonna make a man out of you."

Under Bose's tutelage, Fisher became a top hand for the Goodnight outfit, eventually buying his own ranch and raising his own herd. He and Bose became lifelong friends.

ELEVEN

John Wesley Iliff, his reputation as a cattleman growing, visited the Apishapa ranch in the middle part of the year. After looking over the stock roaming the plains, he dealt with Goodnight over the purchase of the herd. An agreement was reached in which Iliff met Goodnight's price and the Texan committed himself to delivering the longhorns to the Colorado rancher's spread along the Wyoming border before year's end.

Unlike the drive Oliver Loving had made to the Iliff ranch two years previous, Goodnight blazed a new road straight across the plains, avoiding the towns along the South Platte River. The trail was to bear his name for the duration of its use as several Texas cattlemen brought their beeves north to stock the ranges of the upper plains.

After making the delivery and collecting payment, Goodnight decided it was time he had a holiday. He paid the men and at the same time gave them orders to return to the Apishapa two weeks from the day if they wanted to retain employment with him. Most of the men agreed to do so. Those that did also joined their boss on his vacation trip to Denver.

When Iliff paid for the herd, he gave Goodnight two saddlebags filled with hundred-dollar gold pieces, which totalled thirty thousand dollars. The Texan was delighted to have cold, hard cash, but he was also worried about transporting it. That much money would be very inviting to any group of outlaws, and Bill Coe was known to be dogging Goodnight's steps. The ringleader was looking for a chance to avenge himself on the Texan.

Goodnight gathered the men who were going to Denver with him to inform them of the possible danger they might be facing.

"Boys, I'll give it to you straight," he began. He held up the saddlebags containing the gold. "There's thirty thousand dollars here. I happen to know Bill Coe has been following me around, just looking for an opportunity to jump me. We didn't give him one on the way up here, but he might find one while we ride to Denver. There's a good chance there will be some gunplay. I can't ask you to risk your lives to protect my money, so if any of you wish to ride to Denver without me, I will understand."

The five men—Jake Tatum, Frank Willborn, Billy Wilson, Billy Taylor, and Bose Ikard—exchanged questioning looks. Not one of them budged.

"A skunk like Coe don't scare us none," said Billy Wilson. "Besides, we kinda like your company, Mr. Goodnight. Ain't that right, boys?"

"That's right," said Jake. "Y'all don't tell the best stories, Mr. Goodnight, but who cares? Nobody's perfect."

Goodnight couldn't restrain a smile, and the others chuckled.

"Well, I am glad to know I have as much chance of going to Hades as you do, Jake," said Goodnight. There was another chorus of laughter. "Since you all want to risk your necks with me, I'll buy the first round when we reach Denver."

"We got to make it to Denver, boys," said Wilson. "Seein' Mr. Goodnight buy hard liquor is gonna be a once-in-a-lifetime experience, and I sure don't want to miss that."

When the cowboys stopped guffawing, Goodnight added, "Neither do I."

The road to Denver was well worn by the wheels of heavy freight wagons rocking their way to the queen city of the Rockies from the railhead at Julesburg. Most of the route followed the South Platte River. The valley was level, but an occasional hill reached into it from the plain. Those infrequent knolls caused Goodnight some concern, enough for him to take precautions. He would send a man ahead to scout the far side whenever they approached one.

On their second day away from the Iliff ranch, the Texans saw the road rise up and disappear over the horizon. It was Jake's turn to check the other side of the hill. If everything was as it should be, deserted and safe, he was supposed to wave his companions forward. If there was anything that didn't seem right, he was supposed to ride on as if nothing was wrong. The other five men would then circumvent the knoll with their guns ready, hoping to avoid a fight but prepared to shoot it out with anyone who might have thoughts of relieving them of the gold.

Jake casually topped the rise, his head tilted forward as if he were half asleep in the saddle. The others waited fifty yards behind. Tatum's eyes shifted in their sockets as he searched the terrain ahead of him. On each side of the road were trees and bushes big enough to hide a few dozen well-armed men. At first glance, everything seemed to be proper, but then a glint of sunlight off steel caught his attention. He let his horse move on down the far side of the hill.

It had to happen sooner or later, thought Goodnight. He wasn't happy about what might lie ahead, but he was determined to come out on the long end. Without saying a word, he led the four cowboys who remained with him off the roadway. They rode toward a higher place on the knoll, one closer to the plain. It was his intention to view the danger from the best possible vantage point.

When they reached the crest, Goodnight dismounted and handed the reins of his horse to Bose. He knelt low and crept to the top of the ridge. He peered over the edge at the scene below. He counted three men in the trees on the left side of the road. They were armed with rifles, watching the highway. He figured there had to be at least an equal number on the opposite side, probably similarly heeled. He eased his way back to his horse.

"Looks like real trouble down there," he said softly. "It's my guess it's Bill Coe and his bunch. They are looking to jump us, and I would really hate to disappoint them." He unstrapped his side gun and checked the cylinder. The others did likewise. Taking the reins from Bose, he climbed back in the saddle. "Well, let's give them hell, boys."

Each man spurred his horse and they burst over the top of the hill. They held their fire until they were sure they were within range. By that time, the bushwhackers became aware that they were on the defensive.

At the sound of the first shot, Jake turned his mount off the road and jumped to the ground, his rifle in hand. He found cover behind a large boulder with a bush next to it. He drew a bead on an outlaw, then dropped him with the first bullet. He maintained a steady fire throughout the fight.

Goodnight led his men straight through the outlaws, as if he were leading a cavalry charge. The suddenness of the attack worked to their advantage, and Jake's crossfire aided their cause. The Texans emptied their pistols during the initial onslaught, then grabbed their rifles once they were past the ambushers. They leaped from their saddles to seek protection from the few bullets coming at them. Less than a minute later, they ceased shooting when they discovered no one was returning their fire.

"We've had enough, Goodnight," a man's voice shouted at them from the trees.

"Then, come out where we can see you," the cattleman yelled back.

"We can't come out," was the outlaw's reply. "Four of us are dying, and the rest of us are hit."

"Come out unarmed or we'll finish this," said Goodnight.

There was no immediate answer coming from the outlaws. But hardly a moment more passed before two men, one walking and helping the other, who was bleeding from a thigh, emerged from their hiding place. Neither man showed a weapon.

"Don't shoot, Goodnight," shouted the man who appeared not to be injured. "We're unarmed."

"Keep coming this way," ordered the Texan. The two men stumbled closer as they crossed the clearing. "Well, Bill Coe, it is you after all."

"You've shot us to pieces, Goodnight," said Coe, a stout man with a cleft chin.

"You would have done the same to us if given the chance," retorted Goodnight.

"Put me down, Bill," said the man he was helping.

Coe eased him to the ground, then straightened to face the Texans. "I should have known you were too smart to ride into an ambush, Goodnight. With all that money you're carrying, you had to be on the lookout for trouble."

"I have no money with me," said Goodnight.

"What's this?" quizzed Coe.

"Bose, fetch my horse." The black cowboy brought the bay forward. Goodnight took the saddlebags off the animal's back and threw them at Coe. "If you can find any money in there, you are welcome to it."

The outlaw hefted the leather pouches. "Well, there ain't no gold in here." He opened them. "No foldin' cash neither." He eyed Goodnight suspiciously. "I know Iliff paid you before you left his ranch."

"Did he?" Goodnight sat down on a rock. "You can search every man and his horse if you like, Coe." He glared back at his adversary.

"No, I don't think that will be necessary," said Coe.

"How many men did you have, Coe? Five?"

"Countin' me, six."

"Go see if he's telling the truth, Bose. But be careful."

"He's tellin' the truth," said Jake as he walked up to the others. "There's four dead men back there."

"Give this man something to dig with, Bose," said Goodnight. "You're going to bury those men, Coe."

"By myself?"

"All by yourself."

While Coe was digging the graves, Goodnight tended the gaping hole in the injured man's leg. He stopped the bleeding with a pack of river mud, then bandaged the wound. Having seen such injuries before, he knew the man wouldn't be able to ride a horse. He had Jake and Frank make a travois to carry the man to Denver with them.

When Coe finished digging, the Texans laid the four bodies to rest and marked their final resting places with crossed sticks and piles of stones. Goodnight said a few words over them, then turned his attention back to Coe.

"Do you realize what you have done here, Coe? Four men lie dead and this man may lose his leg. All this because you will not work for an honest living. I should hang you myself, but I won't. Instead I am going to let you go your way, because I know once word of this spreads around no man will ever ride with you again.

Your days of outlawing are over, Coe. Now take off your boots."

"My boots?"

"If you don't take them off, I will have my men take them off you."

Coe looked at the determined faces of the Texans. He sat down on a large rock and removed the boots. He handed them over to Goodnight.

"Now, if you show up anywhere with a pair of boots on your feet," said Goodnight, "everyone will know you took them off one of those dead men." Coe looked down at the graves. "Will you become a grave robber now?"

"No, I think not," said the outlaw.

"Then, I think it is time we parted company," said the cowman. "If our paths should ever cross again, I will kill you for certain, Coe."

The Texans mounted their horses and continued their trip to Denver, taking the wounded outlaw with them.

During the final day of the ride to the queen city, Bose took Goodnight aside to ask him the question that was bothering all of the cowboys since their fight with Coe.

"Mr. Goodnight, how come you lied to that man yesterday?"

"How's that, Bose?" queried Goodnight.

"You told him you didn't have no money," said Bose.

"I didn't, Bose," smiled Goodnight. "You had it."

"But I don't understand."

"I told Coe I didn't have the money, and I challenged him to search the rest of us, knowing he wouldn't. I didn't tell him you didn't have the money. I just led him to believe we didn't have any money."

Bose smiled. "Now I understand. You just fooled him, right?"

"That's right, Bose."

The Texans took the injured outlaw to a doctor as soon

as they arrived in Denver. Goodnight paid the physician for his services and left the man in his care.

Oliver Loving had told his partner about the Brown Hotel, and Goodnight had a desire to stay there. He asked the other men to be his guests at the establishment, but all but Bose politely refused the offer. Since Bose was carrying Goodnight's money, it was only natural for him to remain with his employer.

When they reached the hostelry, Goodnight and Ikard went inside to get a room while the others waited on the street. The cowboys had to watch twenty minutes pass before Goodnight and Bose reappeared on the sidewalk.

"Don't be in a hurry, boys," said Goodnight. "I have to take this money over to the bank first."

"That'll take another hour," complained Jake. "A man could die of thirst in that time."

"Well, you can go ahead if you like," said Goodnight.

"Not on your life," emphasized Wilson. "You ain't gettin' out of payin' for the first round of drinks, Charles Goodnight."

"Why, I had no intention of being derelict on my promise," smiled the cattleman.

"That's what I thought," said Wilson. "We'll wait."

An hour later, the six Texans were standing at the bar in the Belmont Saloon. Goodnight slapped a twenty-dollar gold piece on the wooden counter to get the bartender's attention. Since the hall wasn't very crowded, that was an easy task.

"What'll it be, gents?" asked the barkeeper.

"Give these men anything they want until this is gone," said Goodnight, indicating the coin. "For myself, I'll have coffee."

"Same for me," said Bose; then he turned to survey the room.

Only two tables were occupied with card games, five

men at each one. Three miners sat in a corner drinking from beer mugs. Two more men stood at the other end of the bar. Shot glasses rested on the counter in front of them. There wasn't a girl in sight, and this worried the black cowboy.

For months, Bose had let a vision of Hannah dominate his free moments. As Denver came closer, her face became clearer in his mind. He was certain she felt the same about him as he did about her. He hoped he would find out definitely during this stay in Denver.

"Ain't down yet, is she, Bose?" asked Jake.

"What you say, Jake?" asked Bose, pretending he hadn't heard.

"That little gal y'all been seein' when we come to Denver," said Jake, "she ain't around yet, is she?"

"Don't see her, do you?"

"What's this?" asked Goodnight.

"Oh, Bose been keepin' company with a pretty little gal named Hannah every time we come to Denver," explained Jake. "He acts like a lovesick puppy every time he sees her."

Bose intended to deny the allegation, but Hannah's appearance at the top of the stairs kept him silent. She was wearing the same purple satin dress she'd worn the last time he saw her. Her hair was the same, but there was something different. She appeared to be older, much older.

"There she is," said Jake to Goodnight.

The cattleman turned to look at Hannah. "Yes, I see. I can also see why Bose is taken with her."

Hannah saw Bose standing at the bar. She permitted herself a smile but quickly changed to a frown. She looked away from him, but it was too late. Bose was already on his way to the bottom of the staircase to meet her. Slowly, she descended the steps.

"Hello, Hannah," said Bose, a wide smile accompanying his greeting.

"Hello, Bose. I didn't think you was ever coming back."

"I said I was, didn't I?"

"I thought I told you not to come back," she retorted.

"You didn't mean that," said Bose.

"No, I guess I didn't," she admitted. "How have you been?"

"I been fine." Some laughter behind him reminded Bose that they weren't alone. "I got money. Can we go somewheres?"

"To talk?"

"To talk," he concurred.

"Come on," said Hannah as she took his hand to lead him up the stairs. "We might as well go up to my room."

Bose hesitated to go. "Can't we go some other place?"

Hannah glared at him. "I ain't allowed to go out during working hours, and this is working hours."

"But you can go out when you ain't workin'?"

Hannah didn't answer immediately. She stood there peering into his eyes, wondering what he had in mind.

"You can, can't you?" asked Bose again.

"Come on upstairs and we'll talk about that," said Hannah.

They climbed the carpeted steps to her room. Hannah went in first. As soon as they were inside, she held out her hand, and Bose dug into his pocket for some money. He held out a palm full of coins, and Hannah picked out the right amount.

"Now, what have you got on your mind, man?" she asked as she sat down on the bed.

Bose sat down next to her. "I was wantin' to take you for a ride in a buggy."

"A buggy ride? With me?"

"Yes'm. I was gonna rent a fancy rig and take you for a

ride someplace away from here. Maybe we could take along a lunch."

"You really mean that, don't you?"

"Sure I do," smiled Bose.

"Bose," she clucked, "don't you know what I am?"

"We talked about that before." His expression became serious. "Hannah, I don't care what you are when I am away from you. I only care about what you are when we are together. Like right now. I know deep inside you there is a decent woman who wants a man and a family all her own."

"And you're that man?" she interrupted.

"I could be, if you would just give me a chance."

"Uh-hunh. And you're going to take me away from this?"

"Hannah, I love you," Bose blurted out. "I'll take you away from here if you will go."

"And what are you going to take me away to?"

"Back to Texas," said Bose. "My folks got a farm down home now, and I can work it with my pappy. We can live with my folks till we get a place of our own built. I know my mammy would love to have you."

Hannah took Bose's hand in hers. "Bose, it ain't that easy."

"Sure it is. Mr. Goodnight says we're goin' back to Texas right after Christmas, and we're gonna take a wagon. You can ride in the wagon with me."

"No, Bose, that ain't what I meant," she argued. "Getting from here to Texas would be the easy part. It's getting away from here that is hard."

"You ain't no slave no more, Hannah," said Bose sternly. "Ain't no one can tell you when you can go and what you can do."

"Bose, I just can't leave here. I just can't."

"Don't you want to go with me, Hannah?"

With soft hands, Hannah caressed his face. She put her lips to his. Bose permitted the tenderness without returning it. He wasn't sure if he knew how.

"Bose, I would go anywhere in this world with you if I could, but I can't. Don't you see, Bose? This man I work for has got a hold on me."

"What you mean?"

"I owe the man money, and I can't leave till I pay it back."

"How much money you owe this man?"

"More than you got," said Hannah flatly. "I owe him over three hundred dollars."

"How you get to owe him that much money?"

"He charges me for staying here and for eating here and for the clothes I have. I work to pay him back, and sometimes I get part of it paid back. Then the customers don't come around as often, and I get right back where I was before."

"I'll get the money for you, Hannah." He stood up to leave. "Then you can go with me to Texas."

"Don't leave yet, Bose," said Hannah as she grabbed his hand.

"I'll be back," he said as he squeezed her hand. Then, as an afterthought, he pulled her up to him, surrounding her with his arms. "Don't you worry none, Hannah. You're goin' back to Texas with me." He kissed her as best as he knew how to kiss a woman, then left her abruptly.

Goodnight was gone from the Belmont when Bose came downstairs. The other four Texans were still at the bar drinking up the rest of their boss's twenty dollars. Bose went straight to them.

"Well, that was a quick one," said Billy Wilson, who then let out a loud guffaw.

Bose ignored the remark. "Jake, where's Mr. Goodnight?"

Knowing how Bose felt about Hannah, Jake wasn't laughing at Wilson's joke. "I think he went back to the hotel, Bose."

Bose nodded, then left without saying good-bye.

Goodnight was pulling off his boots when Bose entered their room. The black cowboy was obviously agitated over something, as he came straight to the point.

"Mr. Goodnight, I need three hundred dollars."

Goodnight stopped tugging at the boot and straightened up, quite taken aback by Ikard's statement. He looked Bose in the eyes, searching for an answer to the question he was about to ask.

"That's a lot of money, Bose. What do you want it for?"

"I want to get married," said Bose matter-of-factly.

"That's a very serious step in a young man's life," lectured Goodnight. "Is it that girl at the saloon?"

"Yessir," said Bose as he braced himself for a stern talk about the virtues of saloon girls.

"Can't say that I blame you for wanting to marry her, Bose. She is a very lovely young lady. Are you planning on staying here in Colorado?"

Surprised by Goodnight's line of conversation, Bose relaxed some. "No, sir."

"Good. You should go back to Texas, where there's more of your own people. I understand your family has a farm near Weatherford. It might do well for you to take up farming when we get back there. It's a good, solid life, and I know you would be a success at it. You could even raise some cattle, build up a herd of your own."

"Mr. Goodnight, I promised Mr. Lovin', the Lord rest his soul, that's what I'd do," said Bose.

"I know, Bose," said Goodnight softly as he thought of his late partner. "Mr. Loving thought quite highly of you, and I do too. He made me make him a promise too, and that was to help you get started in a different life. That's why I'm going to give you the money. As soon as the bank opens in the morning, we'll go get it. How's that, Bose?"

"That's real fine, Mr. Goodnight," said Bose, astounded by it all.

"Good. Now you had best go back to your young lady and tell her the news. I'm certain she will be happy to hear it."

"Yessir, Mr. Goodnight."

The Texas cowman smiled and nodded, and Bose left for the Belmont.

Evening had settled on the city. The saloons were filling up as working men finished their day of labor and sought refreshment. The Belmont was crowded when Bose burst through the swinging doors.

The hall was full of smoke, and the noise was near deafening. Bose blinked a few times as he adjusted his eyes to the bright lights. He saw his four friends in the exact same spot they were in when he left. They didn't notice him come in. Then he saw Hannah sitting at a table with a white man, a cowboy like himself. He went straight to them.

"Hannah, I got some good news," said Bose as he leaned on the table in front of her.

The girl looked nervous.

"Hannah?" said the white cowboy. "I thought your name was Ebony."

"Her name is Hannah," said Bose harshly. "Ain't no one gonna call her Ebony no more." Then he turned back to Hannah. "Let's go upstairs and talk."

He felt a hand on his arm. "She ain't goin' nowhere with you, nigger."

Bose shook himself free and backed away from the table. His hand instinctively went for his gun.

"No, Bose!" screamed Hannah.

The sudden shriek quieted most of the men in the immediate vicinity, but the roar of the Colt brought silence to the whole room.

The white cowboy had pushed the table away from him and started to come to his feet. At the same time, he reached for his weapon. He never got it clear of the holster. Bose's bullet pierced his chest and ripped a gaping hole in his back when it exited. The cowboy was thrown against the wall behind him, a blank expression in his eyes. He slumped to the floor.

Hannah screamed again.

Then, as suddenly as they had all gone quiet, everyone in the hall was moving for cover.

The bartender reached under the counter for a shotgun. Just as he had it in view, the barrel of a revolver kissed his temple.

"I'd put that back if I was you," Jake said as he clicked the hammer in place. The man complied without argument. "We better get him out of here, boys."

The other three Texans drew their pistols to warn off anyone who had thoughts of interfering. Billy Taylor grabbed Bose by his gun arm. Ikard pulled away, taking aim at his friend.

"Come on, Bose," pleaded Taylor, "we got to get out of here."

The realization of what he had done finally struck Bose. He had killed a man, a white man, and that meant hanging to a Negro, no matter what the circumstances might have been.

"Come on, Bose," insisted Taylor.

Bose and his friends backed out of the saloon. People on the street moved out of their way as they mounted up. A policeman came running toward them. He had his gun out and ready to shoot, but when he saw four armed men, he had better thoughts of shooting it out with them. He

stopped abruptly and watched them ride off at a gallop—
out of town, he hoped.

Because civilization was predominant in the city of
Denver, there were no hurried scenes of the sheriff rounding up a posse, then leading it on a wild chase of the
hunted men. Instead, the policeman who had seen the
Texans ride away went into the Belmont and investigated
the incident. After listening to varied reports of the killing, he repeated them to his superior, who then sent word
to law officers in nearby towns via telegraph to be on the
lookout for five Texans, two of them Negro, who were
wanted in Denver for shooting a man.

The Texans didn't know that they were not being pur-
sued. They made their way out of the city, not stopping
until they were a good five miles away.

"Y'all are the dumbest nigger I ever did see," said Jake.
"How come you had to kill that man? He wasn't botherin'
no one. Why didn't you just whup him with yer fists?" He
shook his head. "Dumb nigger."

"Never mind that now," said Billy Wilson. "It's too late
to change things. We best get back to the ranch as fast as
we can."

"Someone ought to tell Mr. Goodnight what happened," said Bose.

"Bose is right," said Wilson. "I'll go back and tell him.
The rest of you head south for Trinidad. Stay away from
towns and people. You don't know who your friends are
in a time like this."

After taking a breather, the cowboys split up, Wilson
returning to Denver and Jake leading the others to
Trinidad.

It was the middle of the night when Wilson awakened
Goodnight. He quickly recounted the events of the evening. The cowman wasn't pleased, but he was quick to
act.

He went to the telegraph office and awakened the telegrapher. He sent a message to the mayor of Trinidad, saying briefly that friends of his were coming his way and asking the *alcalde* to be of assistance to them. From there, he went to the city marshal's office to see what was being done about the shooting. Goodnight received assurance that justice would be served and the accused killer brought in. That wasn't what he wanted to hear.

Goodnight felt, from Wilson's description, that the shooting wasn't a cold-blooded murder but that it was actually justified in that the dead man had gone for his gun and had provoked Bose to action. For that reason, he was going to do everything in his power to help his hired hand.

With that thought in mind, the Texas cattleman called on the territorial governor. Goodnight's reputation preceded him into the official's office. The governor was effervescent with smiles and handshakes when the Texan entered.

"Mr. Goodnight, this is indeed a pleasure, sir," said the governor. "Indeed a pleasure."

"Governor," said Goodnight simply as he allowed himself to be guided to a chair.

"Please be seated, Mr. Goodnight," said the governor. Then the little man raced around his huge desk and seated himself in a large leather chair, which seemed to swallow him. "Now, sir, what can I do for you?"

"There was a shooting last night in a saloon," said the Texan, coming directly to the matter of his visit. "One of my wranglers shot a man dead over a saloon girl. My man was provoked into the fight. His hand was the surer, and now he is being hunted for the killing. It is my opinion that my man acted in self-defense, and therefore, he should be permitted to go about his business."

"I assume he is in custody," said the governor as he weighed the seriousness of the moment.

"No, he is on the run."

"I see." The governor leaned back in his chair, rolling his eyes toward the ceiling. "If your man is innocent, why is he running?"

"He is a Negro," said Goodnight flatly.

"I see," said the governor, his Yankee conscience coming to the fore. "And you say this man of yours was provoked?"

"Yes."

"That is good enough for me," said the governor. "I will speak with the marshal immediately." He rose from his chair, as did Goodnight. He came around the desk again. "This matter will be cleared up immediately, Mr. Goodnight."

"Thank you, Governor," said Goodnight, shaking the little man's hand. He left the office confident that the incident was closed.

The governor kept his word, and law officers were called off the trail of the Texans. Goodnight continued his vacation in Denver, and his men returned to the Apishapa ranch.

TWELVE

Bose slipped quietly out of the bunkhouse. He was sure he hadn't disturbed any of the other cowboys. He made his way to the stable.

It was well after midnight, and the sky was moonless. He searched in the dark for a halter. He found one, then another, both draped over the top rail of the corral fence. He climbed into the pen with the horses. They moved away from him toward the back of the enclosure. Bose tried to calm them with coaxing whispers.

"Easy there, hoss. It's just me. Ol' Bose. Easy, hoss."

The animals held their ground, each watching him suspiciously. He moved among them. He found his mare and slid one halter over her nose. He led her to the fence and tied the reins to it. He went back for another mount.

Within minutes, he had the second horse and his own saddled and ready to ride. Before he could mount up, he heard footsteps coming his way. He turned around to see a tall figure approaching.

"Little early to start work, isn't it, Bose?" queried Charles Goodnight as he came close to the black cowboy. "Someone going with you?"

"No, sir," said Bose as he stood erect and faced his employer. He was determined not to be deterred.

"Just as I thought." Goodnight had on his heavy winter coat but no hat. His hands were tucked in the pockets. He pulled out his left, a wad of bills folded in it. With the other, he peeled off three one-hundred-dollar notes. After pausing, he took a fourth. He handed them to Bose. "You will probably need this to take care of your business."

Bose was amazed by Goodnight's insight. Hesitantly, he reached for the money.

"I got to do this, Mr. Goodnight."

"I know. Just be careful and bring back my horse."

"Yessir."

Goodnight extended his hand. "Good luck, Bose."

Bose accepted the grip. "Thank you, sir."

"Get going, now. You only have ten days before we leave for Texas."

"Yessir."

Bose climbed into the saddle, nodded at Goodnight, who returned the gesture, then nudged the mare with his heels. She moved away from the Apishapa ranch with the second horse in tow.

Bose had moped around the spread only half interested in his duties ever since the Texans returned from Denver. It was clear to everyone what was troubling the young man, but no one had a solution to his problem. Bose finally arrived at the answer as he listened to Goodnight and Billy Wilson chat idly on the porch of the main house the evening before. Wilson had opened the conversation by mentioning he was tired of punching cows.

"What will you do instead?" asked Goodnight.

"I got two brothers who have a freight company," said Wilson. "They been after me to join up with them. Guess I'll give it a try. Don't know if I'll like it, but I won't know that until I see what it's all about."

"Can't say that I blame you," said Goodnight. "I have sometimes thought of giving up this business, but I am not certain what I would do in its stead. I am certainly not a farmer, and I do not particularly care for the life of a banker or storekeeper. I like the freedom of the range, but I can't help but feel that something is missing."

"A woman," said Wilson simply.

Goodnight stared at him. "A woman?"

"That's right. You ain't got no one to come home to. You need a woman to come home to at the end of the trail."

Goodnight stroked his chin as he mulled over the idea. "Hm-m. You just might be right, Billy."

"I know I'm right. You oughta do somethin' about that problem real soon."

"I just might do that as soon as we get back to Texas. There is a young lady who has caught my eye on more than one occasion. We have spoken of the future, and she has never said anything adverse about living the ranch life. I wonder if. . . ."

His voice trailed off as he decided to keep further speculations to himself.

"What was that?" asked Wilson as he tried to coax the cowman into committing himself.

"Nothing, Billy."

"Don't tell me that," Wilson goaded him. "You was thinkin' about the lady."

"What if I was?" Goodnight was a little indignant.

Wilson shrugged.

"I was just thinking that as soon as we return to Texas I shall approach the lady. There is one problem. I think she is living with relatives in another state."

"So?"

Annoyed by the intrusion into his private thoughts, Goodnight snapped, "So I think I will go after her and damn the consequences."

Goodnight's last declaration stuck in Bose's mind. It was the seed his fertile mind needed to grow a solution to his own problem. He wanted Hannah, but until that moment, he didn't know how he was going to get her.

His attitude changed immediately. Everyone noticed it,

Goodnight especially. He was cheered by it at first, then his curiosity was aroused as he wondered why the sudden turnabout.

He watched Bose closely throughout the day, at last figuring what the black cowboy had on his mind. When he heard the horses milling around in the stable late that night, he knew for certain that Bose was going back to Denver. He knew he couldn't stop him, so he thought it best to help him.

Three days later, Bose arrived in the outskirts of the queen city of the Rockies. The sun was below the peaks in the west. A cold breeze blew in the cowboy's face. He pulled his head deeper into the turned-up collar of his sheepskin jacket, the top button of it having popped off during the trip.

A lamplighter was making his rounds along a residential street. He paused from his nightly routine as Bose approached.

"Cold, ain't it?" offered the man in the long black coat. A stocking cap was pulled down over his ears. He held his lighting stick to one side as he stood beside the pole whose lamp he had just ignited.

Bose halted his horse next to the old man. "Sure is."

"Gonna get colder before the night's over," said the lamplighter, also a Negro though much lighter-skinned than Bose. "I can feel it in my bones. It gonna be a real cold night. Might snow."

"You think so?"

"Cold enough. Can't rightly tell though. Ain't too good at predictin' snow. Real good at rain. Hardly ever wrong there. Ain't missed a rain in near three years. Snow's different thing. Ain't the same as rain. Can't always be sure about it." He tilted his head to one side, his eyes squinted at Bose. "Ain't I seen you before?"

"Doubt it," said Bose, nervous about the inquisitive stare he was receiving.

"Yeah, I seen you before. You the one what kilt a man at the Belmont last month. Saw you come out with a bunch of white cowboys and ride off lickety-split. What you doin' back here? You lookin' to get hung?"

"What you talkin' about, old man?"

"Don't you know who you kilt that night?"

"Just a white cowboy."

The lamplighter laughed. "Just a white cowboy. If that was all he was, ain't no one would make a fuss."

Bose was baited. "Who was he?"

"Name was Hal Robbins. His brother be Jack Robbins, the man what owns the Belmont. He swear he gonna kill you if you ever come back to Denver." He studied Bose for a moment, looking for signs of fear. He found none. "You wasn't headin' back there, was you?" Bose didn't answer. "Robbins says he gonna hang you himself, 'cause the law won't do nothin' about you killin' his little brother. He says he gonna hang you from the sign over the door."

"Is that so?"

"That's what the man say."

"Well, I guess I better see if Mr. Robbins is a man of his word."

Bose urged his horse into a walk.

"Don't say I didn't warn you," the old man called to him. "Don't want you dead on my conscience."

"I'll be sure to tell St. Peter you did your best to save me," said Bose over his shoulder. Then, under his breath, he added, "If I get to the pearly gates before you, ol' man."

The chance meeting and subsequent conversation certainly muddled Bose's plan. He originally determined that he would confront Hannah's boss and offer him the money she owed. He was certain the man would accept and let Hannah go with him back to Texas. Now that he knew her employer was the brother of the man he had killed, he wasn't sure what to do. Going to the Belmont while it was open for business was out. In fact, going anywhere near there while people were about was eliminated from his plan.

"Just have to go when there ain't no one around," he muttered to himself.

He decided to lie low until the town was asleep. He found an alley behind the business district. He rode into it and dismounted. He sat down in a corner, out of the wind. He tied the reins of his horse around his ankle and settled himself for a nap. In a few minutes, the fatigue of the trail caught up with him and he slumbered.

A solid knock on the sole of one boot awakened the black cowboy hours later. He drew the leg back and reached for his gun at the same time.

"Don't move, nigger," said a hard voice. A hammer click reinforced the order. Bose stayed motionless. "That's better. Now on your feet."

Bose came erect. On the way up, he caught the gleam of a polished metal badge. Once straightened, he saw that he was confronting a Denver policeman.

"What are you doing back here, boy?" asked the lawman.

"Just sleepin'," said Bose.

"With two horses?"

"They're both mine."

"I'll bet they are," said the officer sarcastically. "Where you from, boy?"

"Down Trinidad way. Work for Mr. Goodnight over on the Apishapa."

"Cowboy. I should have known." He peered at Bose inquisitively. "Wait a minute. Did you say Goodnight?"

"Yessir."

"Then, you must be that nigger who killed young Hal Robbins last month." Bose's eyes widened as he feared what was coming next. "I thought so. Jack is going to be real happy to see you." The policeman motioned with his revolver. "That way, nigger."

Bose didn't move. "Can I untie my hoss's reins from my ankle?"

The officer looked down at the knot, then nodded his approval. Bose bent down. He loosened the bindings, then lunged head first into the lawman's midsection.

"Oo-ooh!" grunted the policeman as he was sent sprawling across the alley. His gun flew out of his hand and discharged when it hit a wall. The shot echoed between the buildings.

Bose jumped on the breathless man. He doubled his fist and slugged him as hard as he could. For good measure, he repeated the blow. Bose made sure the officer was still breathing, before rising. The lawman didn't move, but he was alive.

Fortunately, the horses hadn't run off. Bose grabbed the reins of his mare and leaped into the saddle. He knew someone would be coming along to see what the commotion was. He kicked the mare in the ribs and galloped down the alley to the street. In a minute, he was three blocks away, turning onto the avenue where the Belmont had its address. He slowed his mount as he made his way toward that establishment.

The saloon had a straight-up-and-down front. Two windows, one on each side of the door, graced the first story and four the second level. The sign advertising the name of the place stuck out over the boardwalk from the peak of the frontispiece. There was no balcony. There was an alley on the right of the building, and a stairway left from it to a door on the top floor. Bose knew that was his entrance.

He turned into the alley. He climbed down and tied the mare to the railing on the landing of the staircase. Slowly, he ascended to the upper level.

He was in luck. The door was unlocked. He opened it and walked into a darkened hall. He stood motionless for a few minutes as he waited for his eyes to adjust to the blackness. When he felt he could make out any objects that might be in his way, he took a short step forward. Then another. He wasn't sure he could find Hannah's room from that direction, so he stole down the hall until he came to the inside stairs. He took his bearings, then went for her door.

It, too, was not locked. He turned the knob slowly, trying to avoid making any noise. There was none. He took a step inside, and he would have continued if a creak from a floorboard hadn't stopped him.

"Who's there?" he heard Hannah demand. Her words were followed by the sound of a gun being cocked.

"It's me, Hannah. Bose Ikard." His voice was a whisper.

Hannah jumped out of bed and grabbed the door and Bose at the same time. She closed the door and pulled him inside with a single motion.

"Are you crazy?" she asked in hushed anger.

"I come to get you, Hannah." Bose was sure that would please her. It didn't.

Hannah turned up the flame in the lamp beside her bed just enough to give the room a dim illumination.

"You are crazy," she said. "I can't go with you."

Bose pulled out the money Goodnight had given him. "Sure you can. I got the money to pay Robbins what you owe him. See?" He waved the money at her.

She grabbed the bills and threw them on the bed.

"There ain't enough money in the world that could bring back Mister Robbins' brother, the man you shot."

Bose glared at her. "That can't be changed. The man went for his gun. Besides, he was touchin' you."

"Lots of men touched me before him and since," Hannah retorted.

"No one but me ever gonna touch you again."

"Who says?"

Bose grabbed her by the shoulders and jerked her close to him. "Hannah, I love you, and you love me, don't you?"

Hannah's first reaction was to resist, but the fight went out of her as quickly as it had come. She went limp in his strong hands.

"Yes, Bose," she whispered, "I do love you."

"Then, get your things together. We're goin' to Texas."

"But I—"

He squeezed her harder. "Hannah, you're gonna be my wife, and I'm gonna be your man. A woman got to learn to do what her man say." There was silence between them. "Do you understand?"

"Yes, Bose," she said, half frightened, half filled with joy.

He thought about releasing her, but his love for her overwhelmed him. He pulled her against him, kissing her hard with the passion he had previously denied. He didn't notice how she returned the endearment.

Suddenly, the door burst open.

Jack Robbins, his pale face contrasted by a black beard and hair, stood there in the doorway holding a six-shooter aimed in Bose's direction.

Bose pushed Hannah away from him onto the bed. She screamed. The black cowboy went for his gun, spinning around as he did to face Robbins.

"You!" said Robbins, surprised to see the man he hated and wanted to hang.

Without thinking, Bose fired his Colt at the same instant Robbins pulled his trigger. The two shots resounded as one, and both bullets hit flesh.

The gun fell from Bose's hand as he reeled from the wound, falling backward across Hannah. Robbins crashed into the wall opposite the doorway. Hannah screamed again when she was splattered with blood.

A groan escaped the cowboy's lips as he rolled off the bed onto the floor. Hannah grabbed for him but was too late to halt his body from collapsing on the carpet. His hat, knocked askew by the fury of his movements, finally fell off his head. His eyes were glassing.

"Bose!" cried Hannah as she knelt beside him.

The sound of her voice rousted his deepest reserves of strength. The pain in his right shoulder slapped hard at his senses, furthering his efforts to remain conscious. He reached for the wound, a small hole below the clavicle, a gory mixture of skin, muscle, blood, wool, and leather where the slug exited between his armpit and shoulder blade. His fingers felt his own hot, wet blood.

"Hannah, stop the bleedin'," he said hoarsely. "You got to stop the bleedin'."

She ripped her gown at the hem, tearing loose a large piece of the white cloth. Bose had unbuttoned his coat at the same time. He rolled over, his head coming to a rest face down on her lap. She stuffed the cotton material inside his coat against the wound. Bose turned over again.

"Now button my coat," he ordered her.

She obeyed.

With his left hand, Bose retrieved his gun. He pushed himself erect with Hannah's aid. He stumbled toward the hall. He rocked against the doorway, the light from the room silhouetting him. He stepped out of the room and to one side to let the dim glow illuminate the passageway. He trained the Colt on the man slumped on the floor, his back propped against the wall.

"Who was he?" asked Bose.

"Jack Robbins," said Hannah as she joined him.

The saloon owner was dead. A gaping hole with a trickle of blood coming from it was barely visible above his solar plexus.

"Well, he can't stop you now, Hannah."

There were voices in the street. A scream came from down the hall. Bose looked up to see two other women in their nightclothes watching the scene. One slapped the other.

"Shut up, you!" she snapped before pushing her back into her room. Then she moved cautiously toward Bose and Hannah. "You'd better get out of here. You, too, Hannah. Neither one of you'll live to see daylight if you don't."

"Bose is hurt," Hannah argued.

"It ain't bad," said Bose. "She's right, Hannah. We got to get."

Hannah's eyes searched the other woman's, then Bose's. Her decision was made. She went back into her room. She didn't trouble herself with packing anything. She slipped into a dress and a pair of shoes. She wrapped herself in a greatcoat and pulled the blanket off the bed. The four one-hundred-dollar bills fell on the floor. She grabbed them and stuffed them into a pocket.

"Let's go," she said as she joined Bose in the hall.

Her friend was standing at the door to the alley stairs.

"It's clear," she said. She held the door open for them. "Good luck."

"Thanks," said Hannah as she touched her friend's hand in gratitude and farewell.

Hannah helped Bose down the steps.

K26

"Get up on that one," said Bose as he motioned to the second horse with his head.

"I ain't never rode a horse before," she said, a touch of panic in her voice.

"Just put your foot in there," he said, pointing at the stirrup, "and pull yourself up by the horn." She did as she was instructed. "Now hold onto the horn and hold on tight."

The second horse was still tied to his mare by a lead rope. He climbed onto his mount slowly, using only his left hand to pull himself up.

"Hang on tight, now," he commanded Hannah once more. Then he kicked his horse into action.

They rode down the alley to another one that was perpendicular with it. Bose turned the mare to the right. He heard someone shout in the street behind them.

"Let's get, hoss!" he said as he spurred the animal beneath him. She broke into a gallop, and they were away.

In a half hour, they were on the road to Trinidad, and there was no one following them.

EPILOGUE

"Did they get away, Grandpappy?" asked Rafer.

"Co'se they did," said the old man.

"Did they get back to Texas?" asked Tommy.

"Co'se they did. But they went to New Mexico first. Mr. Goodnight had one mo' promise to keep to Mr. Lovin'. He promised him befo' he died that he would bury him in Texas. Mr. Goodnight and all the cowboys took Mr. Lovin' back to Texas with 'em and buried him in the land he loved."

"What happened to Bose and Hannah?" asked Tommy.

"Bose? He give up bein' a cowboy. He and Hannah got married and had a fam'ly. They become farm folks."

"Was he ever a cowboy again?" asked Rafer.

"Nope. Lived all the rest of his days on the farm."

"Gee, that was really a neat story, Grandpappy. Tell us another one, will you?"

"That's 'nough fo' today," said the old man. "Y'all go on and play now."

"Aw, gee," moaned the boys.

"Go on, now," insisted the old man.

"Come on, Rafer," said Tommy, "let's play cowboys and Indians again."

"Okay," said Rafer, "but this time you're the Indian and I'm gonna be the cowboy."

They walked away to continue their make-believe drama.

The old man rocked in his chair, nodding his approval.